xoxo

# Fan is a Four Letter Word

D1526251

a novel by Eidora Dene

XOXO

# İçerikler

# PROLOGUE

*And That's All I Have To Say About That!*
*All Things EverMorph All the Time*

Season 4 Episode Highlights - performance of Liam Caffney and Marnie Wethers. Lowlight - Story continuity!!!

*Alright you Everrites and Morphlings, Holy Hanna! The Fae are looking down upon this week's episode and are weeping! And not those good happy tears of "Yes! Preach our story!" but rather the sad angry tears of "What in the universal realms was that?!"*

*Okay, now to be fair there were some brilliant and masterful moments between Lochlan and Beatrice. The way Lochlan is trying to save even a small part of humanity and his blooming love for Beatrice that he is desperately trying to fight is coming through in the most beautiful inflections of the voice and subtle* movements of his body. And you can see Beatrice fighting it as well. All her indecision is right there in her eyes! Almost had me in tears! Ah, but the rest of the show was truly cringe worthy. Why you may ask? Well, let me tell you. But first let me ask you a question. Did the show get some new writers? Did they have a junior writer on staff they figured they would give a shot to? Listen, I'm all for giving a newbie a chance. We need to open the writing field. But by the Goddess of Nyla put them on a very short leash! They MUST have some guidance, a senior writer to make sure they don't royally screw up! I watched no less than three instances where characters said the exact same lines as other characters from another season! VERBATIM! I kid you not!! What what? Come on! Continuity people! Let's keep some! Follow the story and be true to it! Do your research! If you need a script supervisor, I'm available. A keeper of history, a continuity nazi if you will, then I'm your gal! Call me! I'll come running (well, not running, because I hate running. But a speedy walk I'll give you)

And dear readers if you are scratching your head wondering what possible moments I could be talking about, well here you go. If you would be so kind as to look up these times on season 4 episode 8 - 15:12, 28:04, and 42:04 against season 2 episode 3 - 4:15,20:20 and 34:38. You too will be saying "Holy Fae-nal!"

Alright EverMorph Universe talk to me! Share your thoughts about my thoughts. What insights do you feel should be recognized from this episode? I want to hear it all!

Until next time EternallyEvers OUT!!

*Comments:* **Morphing4Oberon** *:* *Holy Hanna is right EterenallyEvers! I bet someone's head is rolling soon and not just because Rogan wants to start a war! Great catch!!*

**LochlanisMine:** *You did it again EE nice catch! You'd make a great script supervisor, although I'm sure some of the writers would disagree LOL*

**MorphlingsWillRise:** *Damn EE! Be nice! I'm sure some newbie is crying in o his script as I type this!*

**NylaKingdom4Ever:** *EternallyEverly have you ever thought about writing a fanfic for EverMorphs? I think it would be fabulous!*

* * *

Abigail smiled as the comments on her blog started rolling. She loved that her followers started commenting almost immediately after she posted something. It was as satisfying as an eager student raising their hands when she asked a question. Smiling, she closed her laptop. Tomorrow was an early day, which meant tonight needed to be an early night.

# CHAPTER ONE

Abigail's short heels clicked against the newly polished floors as she headed to her classroom. Tomorrow would be the first day back from Christmas break, and she wanted to rearrange the desks. No matter how many times she changed them around, the cleaning crew always put them back into standard formation when they were done cleaning. This time she had waited until they had finished with her room before starting the change. Her seniors would be starting a new section in the morning, and true to form she always did a new room configuration when a new section was beginning. This time it would be *Chaucer's Canterbury Tales*.

She flipped the lights on and put her bag down on the desk. She put her long black braids up in a bun and started moving desks into two octagons with a center space for her to teach from if she wanted to. Abigail needed to make the center space a little large. As a plus size woman she made the world adjust to her, not the other way around. It had taken her some time, but she loved every inch of her mocha brown body. All the curves, lumps, bumps, and dimples equaled love. It was who she was and she refused to apologize for it. Abi was quick to cut people out of her life who tried to change her, well meaning or not. Those who tried to lead her down a path of what they believe would be a healthier, thinner, and therefore happier life. They found themselves looking at her back and hips as she sashayed away from their lives.

Once the new room design was done, she pulled fresh folders out of her bag. One for every student. Inside held the syllabus for the new unit, a pack of blank college ruled paper, a list of resources that would help her students study and understand Chaucer better, and of course five self-designed stickers. It was her trademark. Homemade stickers that exemplify the feelings her students may exhibit while diving into the material. This particular unit had WTF?!? coming out as steam from a cup of coffee, an exploding head with My head hurts coming out the top, and one with two cats walking opposite directions but their tails were entwined and underneath it read Keep Calm and Read On. Next to last was a year calendar with a red circle around a date. Above it was the word Done! The very last sticker in the collection never had to do with the unit of material. It was always a secret homage to her favorite television show *The EverMorphs*. It was two moons with the shadow of fairy wings behind the second moon. It was so subtle. So subtle that most of her students would think it was an eclipse because they knew Miss. Reese loved astronomy. What they didn't know is that it was an insignia Abi had come up with to represent The House of Nyla. They were the ruling family in *EverMorphs*.

It gave her a warm giggle to know she was secretly sharing a small part of herself with her favorite humans. And such a big secret it was, only her best friend Tess and her online community knew; with them she openly shared her love of *The EverMorphs*, but even they did not know her true identity, only her online persona. It was safe and she could freely share so much of herself with like minded people without ever worrying about repercussions.

Abigail had her reasons for keeping this part of herself a secret. She had seen enough online videos and interviews with celebrities talking about "their fans". Abi was an observer, not only of words but of actions and movements. Celebrities could verbalize how much they *loved* their fans as much as they wanted, but their body language and ticks often betrayed their proclamations of love, leaving a question mark about their true feelings. Abigail could always pick up on it. It was the one area actors were terrible at acting about.

With the folders on the desks, she took a final look around the room and nodded in satisfaction. She grabbed her bag as she flipped off the lights and headed for home. Tomorrow was going to be an interesting day.

* * *

Liam collapsed onto his couch as he took a deep calming breath. It had been a long day on set, but a good one. Only four more episodes needed to be filmed for the season. So that meant three, maybe four more months of shooting. Arlene, his agent, had sent over a pile of scripts that would fit into his off-season time and still leave several weeks of complete downtime before *EverMorphs* started filming season nine. He looked at the pile, deciding he needed a snack before jumping into the fray. He stood, letting his long legs stretch as he headed to the kitchen. Putting the water filled kettle on the stove, he blended several different types of tea leaves to make his own blend of chai tea. While he waited for the kettle to boil, he fixed himself a grilled cheese and tomato sandwich. It was an indulgence that usually wasn't on his "show diet" but it was what he was craving so he allowed himself to indulge. It was one of his rules. Life was too short not to indulge every now and then.

Sandwich and tea in hand he headed back to the living room. Making himself comfortable with his legs folded underneath him, he put his long, dark curls back into somewhat of a bun. He took a bite of his sandwich and started flipping through the pile just looking at the titles. He knew he would read all of them, but for now he was looking for a title that would grab his attention. As he came close to the bottom of the pile and finished off his sandwich, he stopped at *Hidden Tales*. Maybe it was the font or just the implication that something was hidden deep within the tales.

Whatever it was, Liam picked up the script and started reading it. He pulled a blanket across his body as he got lost in the script. Time slipped past Liam as he read and then re-read it again. He was nodding his head as he read. This was it, this was the show he wanted. It was a retelling of *The Canterbury Tales*. Modern with a little dark twist. He was intrigued with the part the producers were looking at him for, the pardoner.

He briefly remembered reading *The Canterbury Tales* in high school, but that was so long ago, he liked it then, but that was all he could really remember about the experience. He drained his tea and headed to the shower. He'd called Arlene in the morning. *Hidden Tales* would be a nice change from *The EverMorphs*. He couldn't pass what would be a short commitment for something so new and interesting.

# CHAPTER TWO

———◆———◆———

The next morning Liam called his agent. "Hey Arlene, sorry, I know it's early, but I have to be on set soon. But I wanted you to know I'm really interested in *Hidden Tales*. So whatever needs to happen, let's do it."

Arlene clasped her hands in triumph. "Excellent! I was hoping you would pick that one. I'll get in touch with the producers today. Liam, before I let you go, how do you feel about attending a little fan event?"

Liam rolled his eyes. "Leenie, you know I love my fans but with my schedule, I just don't think—"

No, no, this is a real simple one. It's at an animal shelter. It's more about getting people to adopt than anything else. You'll be spending more time with animals than with fans. Only four hours next Saturday."

"Leenie—"

"Sign some autographs, take a few photos. I thought you loved your fans."

"I am keenly aware that I am where I am in my career not just because of my talent, but because of my fans as well, it's just sometimes they are a little much. Besides, will it even fit into my shooting schedule? We've been shooting quite a few weekends lately."

"Don't get upset, but I already cleared it with the people at *TEM* yesterday. They were gracious enough to make a small change in the shooting schedule so I could whisk you away for two days without completely ruining the shooting schedule or make them go over. Honestly, they were very accommodating. I have a feeling more than one of them has a rescue animal waiting for them at home."

Liam pinched the bridge of his nose and took a deep breath. "Fine Leenie, I'll do it. I'll go to Connecticut in the middle of winter for you. Just email me the details."

Arlene smiled into the phone. "And this is why you're my favorite client, and it's practically Spring really."

"Ha! Spring my ass, it's barely the middle of January." Liam snorted. "I assumed I was your favorite because of the ten percent I keep putting in your pocket."

Arlene laughed, knowing he was kidding. "Tsk, tsk, it's too early to be so cynical. Now go to work and I'll email you about the event and *Hidden Tales*. Ciao for now." Arlene hung up.

Liam put his phone down and headed for the shower. Another long day was waiting for him on set.

* * *

Abigail stepped out of the shower, enveloping herself in a big fuzzy towel and then took her braids out of the bun they had been in. She continued her morning ritual as she listened to some classic rock on Pandora. Five songs later and she was out the door headed to Odyssey High School. Home of the fighting blue sharks.

Abigail had her senior honors English class first period. Several of those students were also in the drama club, of which she was the advisor. She knew those few would probably come up with the most elaborate presentations for the Chaucer section. She was already looking forward to seeing it. She hummed a tune as she walked into her classroom. She was pleased to see that the janitorial staff had not moved her fabulous figure eight. She was writing the first assignment on the board when Margot came in, Margot was one of her favorite students. But she would deny having favorites if anyone asked. She was a chubby girl that in college would either solidify herself as a plus size beauty or slim down to a societal "average" woman. Either way, Abigail hoped she would always be strong in the belief of who she is.

Margot was smiling as she handed Abigail a printout. "Miss Reese, did you see this? I think you should enter. You're a fan of the show, right?"

Abigail took the printout from Margot and read it. *The EverMorphs* were running a nationwide contest for drama students. Abigail sucked in her breath, as she mustered up a smile for Margot. "What would I need with a contest like this? And what exactly is an EverMore? Sounds like something from Edgar Allen Poe."

Margot took the paper back and laughed. "It's *EverMorphs*, Miss Reese, but I have a sneaky suspicion that you know that already."

Abigail just stared at Margot, trying not to reveal anything.

"It's okay Miss Reese, from one Everrite to another, your secret is safe with me." Margot gave her teacher a wink and headed to her desk. She picked up the folder and immediately pulled out the stickers. "I love it when you make us new stickers!"

Abigail relaxed a little. If there was anyone she could talk with about *EverMorphs* and have kept secret would be a person like Margot. But still she needed to keep some things just for herself. "I'm glad you like them. Just remember that when you are rooting through the mind that is Chaucer."

The other students started filing in. Abigail straightened and smiled. "Welcome back from break. I hope you all had some fun and got some rest because we are about to delve into a world you have never been to before. Chaucer's *Canterbury Tales* is a challenge as well as a delight for the mind."

Tanner raised his hand and began speaking. "Do we have to read it in its original form, or do we get to a modern version?"

Abigail pointed to the folder on his desk. "Take out the stickers in the folder and you tell me."

Tanner looked at the stickers and his shoulders slumped as he sighed. "Original form."

Abigail stifled a laugh. "I'll try to make it as painless as possible. This is one of my favorites and hopefully by the time we are done, it will be a favorite of yours too." Abigail started passing out the books. "Now let's dive in, shall we?

*  *  *

Liam smiled at the flight attendant as she handed him a drink. He took a sip then put it down as he picked a copy of Chaucer's *Canterbury Tales*. His deal for the role of the Pardoner wasn't set in stone yet, but he wanted to familiarize himself with the original text the show was derived from. He had bought a copy on Amazon with the original text without the handy modern version on the next page. He figured, why not fully commit? It was his third time reading through the same paragraph in the Pardoner's Tale when he felt a small hand lightly tap his shoulder. He turned to see a little girl with fairy ears on and an Everrite family crest necklace around her neck. She looked scared. She couldn't have been any older than ten. He tried to calm her.

"Well hello there. And what might your name be?"

"My, hi, my name is, are you Lochlan?"

Liam did his best to turn his smirk into a smile. He hated when "fans" couldn't separate the actor from the character. But she was a little girl. Little children were the exception to all his fan rules. Well, the nice ones anyway. He turned to the little girl. "Why yes, I am. And who might you be, my little fairy?"

The little girl giggled. "My name is Stella. You're my favorite!"

"Aren't you the sweetest?" He looked around before leaning close to Stella's ear. "Don't tell Isla, but *you*, Miss Stella, are *my* favorite fairy."

Stella giggled. "Can I please take a picture with you? I need proof, or my friends won't believe me."

Liam ran his fingers through his hair, unbuckled his seatbelt and sat up a little straighter. "Of course darlin' Anything for my favorite fairy."

Stella fumbled with her phone for a moment. She was so nervous.

"Here Stella, let me take the pic. Longer arms and all." Liam wrapped his free arm around Stella, sticking his other arm out into the aisle to get them both in the shot. "Say "Long live Nyla!"

"Long live Nyla!" Stella smiled.

Liam took two pictures and handed the phone back to Stella. Just then her mother came running up the aisle. "Stella! I told you not to bother him!" She turned to Liam. "I am so sorry. I hope she wasn't too much of a bother."

Liam gave his million dollar smile. "No trouble at all. It's always nice to meet another fairy from the realm." Liam winked at Stella.

"Well, we'll let you enjoy the rest of your flight in peace. Won't you, Stella?" The mother gave Stella a little pinch on the arm.

"Sorry to bother you, Lochlan." Stella looked down at the floor.

Liam took her hand and gave it a kiss. "No need to apologize, it was my greatest pleasure to have met you."

The mother gave Stella a gentle shove to make her go back to her seat. She looked back at Liam and waved, then headed back down the aisle. The mother watched her go. "Again, sorry for the trouble."

Liam tipped his glass at her and smiled. Once the mother was gone, he went back to reading. He was frustrated with how long it was taking him to truly digest the reading. If he got the role, he would think about getting a tutor. His interest in Chaucer had been rekindled with the possibility of this role. He closed the book, leaning back against the chair and closing his eyes for the rest of the flight.

Arlene met Liam at the airport. "There he is! My number one client. How was the flight?" She hugged Liam.

"Leenie, what a nice surprise! I wasn't expecting you."

"Well, since I kind of strong-armed you into doing this, I figured I'd better show up and give you some support."

"Ah, you really are a doll. Thanks for coming. I'm ready to face the masses!"

"Slow down there, cowboy. First I'm taking you to dinner. The masses will happen bright and early tomorrow. Come on, let's get you to the hotel and all checked in."

# CHAPTER THREE

❖────────────❖

*And That's All I Have To Say About That!*

*All Things EverMorph All the Time*

## Mid Episode Development Alert!!

*Greetings my favorite fairies. I know it's not my usual blog day, but a little butterfly floated something past me that I had to pass along to my realm. So here we go, I hope you are all sitting down. Our beloved NeverMorph is running a contest. And not just your run of the mill contest. That's good right? Well, you might not think that when I tell you more. Please stop me if you've heard this. Oh, wait you can't. So, if you know what I'm talking about just scroll down and leave a comment on who you think is behind the curtain spying on Lochlan and Beatrice under the moonlight. Which hopefully we will get the answer to on the next episode*

*Now, back to the contest. A proclamation has been called across the kingdom of Nyla. Apparently, the Queen along with her faithful and valiant (not to mention smoking hot) son, Lochlan, are holding a royal contest. To bequeath their glorious attendance at a performance. This contest is for high school drama teachers/ coaches, so if you know any, sound the alarm and bring them into the fold of knowledge! The best royal request as to why the queen and her favorite son should help the drama clan of (insert school name here) will win. The winners will be granted a visit by the queen and her son in person! How to enter the contest and in what form must the request be in? That is a very good question. The rules seem a bit vague but go to the EverMorphs official site to get the true blue lowdown.*

*Now, I have no idea why the show decided to do this. Who knows what the powers that be have going on in their minds. But it's an opportunity for a teacher and her students to be touched by the magic of EverMorphs for a brief time in the cosmos. So sound the trumpets and spread the word. Until the next episode...........*

*EternallyEvers OUT!*

Comments **NylaKingdom4Ever:** *Thanks for the update EE! My best friend is a drama teacher. I'll be passing this along to her. EternallyEvers are you entering?*

> response - **EternallyEvers:** *What makes you think I teach drama ;)*

> **BeatriceBabe:** *I think it's Isla spying on Lochlan and Beatrice. She is just so jellie!*

*RogansRaiders: I think it's one of Rogan's spies. He needs some dirt to get some leverage against Lochlan.*

*IdolofIsla: My students are already working on a presentation fit for royalty! What a great opportunity!!*

*LochlanisMine: Why only drama teachers?! No fair!!*

*response - MorphlingsWillRise: Sorry LochlanisMine, you win some you lose some. If it makes you feel any better, I can't enter either. I think it might be part of a larger campaign to keep the arts alive in the public school systems. There are a couple of other shows from the same streaming service doing similar things.*

*MorphingforOberon: It's gotta be Nyx. She's Isla's first maiden. You all know she thinks Lochlan is cheating on Isla with Beatrice. That little fairy is out for proof. Also, I think she is secretly in love with Isla so.....*

*response: BeatriceBebe: Yes! Nyx totally is in love with Isla! So if it's not Isla directly I can absolutely see Nyx venturing out on her own to learn the truth. I can't wait for the big reveal!*

* * *

Abigail's alarm went off several times before she groaned and rolled over, slapping it to turn it off. She curled back over to catch some more zzz's before she truly had to get up. The sun peeking through the blinds had other ideas. She sighed as she rolled out of bed and down to the kitchen to make herself some cinnamon coffee. She looked out the window and smiled, it was the perfect day for a pet adoption fair. The sun was shining, and the forecast promised no snow and a comfortable temperature, a little above average for January

For the last three years Abigail had been volunteering one Saturday a month at **The Giggles and Cuddles Animal Shelter.** This Saturday was their annual big push for not only adoptions but funds to keep the center going. She looked down at her two treasures, Lochlan and Beatrice. They were mewing for their morning meal. She quickly made their breakfast, gave them a few ear scratches, and headed up to her room to get ready for the day.

Abigail loved the drive to the shelter. It was all back roads filled with open fields and trees. It was only twenty minutes, but it was a serene twenty minutes. She lived a little bit outside of New Haven, in one of Connecticut's smaller towns. It was a dramatic difference from the concrete of Manhattan, and that had been the main draw for her to accept the teaching position at Odyssey High. It was perfect really, she had the greenery and nature she wanted but the small city of New Haven was just a hop, skip and a jump away. And Manhattan was only a short train ride away. It really was the perfect location for her. It made her sigh in contentment just thinking about it.

When she arrived at the shelter, everyone was running around trying to get things ready. Post holiday adoption drives were always the hardest. So many pets had been given as gifts for Christmas and Hanukkah and then brought to the shelter when it wasn't all fun and games for the new owners.

It always frustrated Abigail how people didn't understand the responsibility of a pet until it was too late and it was always the pet who suffered for it. That's why this event was so important and she had a feeling it was going to go very well.

Abigail found the manager to find out where she was needed most. "Hey Steve, where do you need me?"

A look of relief came over his face. "Oh Abi! Thank god, you are here! I need you in the puppy pen today."

"Sure! No problem. Oh, are we doing the twenty five dollar adoption special today?"

"Yes, but there is something more important you need to be doing while in the pen."

"Oh no, Steve! You aren't sticking me with a newbie, are you?"

Steve gave Abigail one of his best smiles. "Kind of, but not really. We have a celebrity here to help boost the adoptions and raise some funds. He'll be spending a good portion of his time here with the puppies because we have more than we can handle at the moment and really need to get some adopted today." Steve rushed his words, not giving himself a breath.

"Breathe, Steve! Alright, I guess. So tell me, who will I be babysitting today?"

Steve's whole body seems to relax. "Oh thank you Abi, I knew I could count on you. I was so afraid to put him with one of the younger volunteers."

"Hey!" Abigail laughed.

"Oh! Sorry, I meant that he's from a popular show and I was afraid they wouldn't be able to control themselves. I know what a scholarly reader you are. I didn't think you would get all loopy around him."

Abigail smiled. "Thanks? I guess. So tell me, who is this guy anyway?"

"His name is Liam Caffney? He's on a show called The EverPeople? No, no, *The EverMorphs*. Have you heard of it?"

Abigail put all of her college acting techniques into action and kept a blank and even keeled look on her face. "I haven't watched it myself, but some of my students talk about it every now and then."

Steve nodded. "That's what I thought. It's more of a teen, early college age type show, right?"

Abigail just nodded.

Steve handed her two shirts. "One for you and one for Liam, he should be here in about fifteen minutes."

Abigail smiled. "Great! That gives me just enough time to change into my shirt and then I'll get the pen ready." She walked off to the bathroom.

Once inside the ladies' room, she checked the stalls to make sure she was alone. Assured of her solitude she did a little happy dance in the bathroom that lasted maybe fifteen seconds before reality crashed in. She was going to be in enclosed space with one of her favorite actors who played her favorite character on her favorite show. He couldn't know she was a fan. She had to keep her cool. But how could she even look him in the eye without gushing over him? Or worse, be stone cold and say nothing? Abigail splashed some water on her face. "Hold it together Abi! You've got this. He's just some guy for a show you like. It's fine. Remember why you are here. It's all about the pups and kitties today," she said to herself as she looked in the mirror and gave herself a reassuring nod.

She splashed some more water on her face and changed her shirt. Looking in the mirror she wished she had put some lipstick on, maybe some eyeliner and mascara before she left the house. She laughed at herself for acting like a giddy schoolgirl. She took several deep breaths to calm herself. She looked through her purse and found a shade of lipstick that was subtle but could be seen. It was what she considered a day shade and it would go well with the coral color in her shirt.

Now that she was composed, she grabbed the shirt for Liam. Staring at it, she smiled. It gave her an idea. She quickly went and found Steve.

"Steve! I have an idea. These shirts, we have a bunch, right?"

Steve nodded. "We've got a couple of boxes full. Why? Do you need another one?"

"No, I mean yes. I mean we should ask this Liam guy to sign some, and then we can sell them. If he's as popular as you say, I bet they will sell out. More money for the shelter, right? Maybe twenty-five or thirty dollars a piece? Is that too much?"

Steve snorted. He looked round then put his arm around Abigail. "Between you and me, I'm a huge science fiction fan.

I haven't watched his show, but I've been to conventions where his show has had panels. Their merch is super expensive and sells out almost every time."

"So good! Let's do twenty- five for pre-signed and forty-five for personalization? Wait, do you think he would do it?"

Steve smiled. "Only one way to find out. Here he comes now."

Abigail turned as Liam and a woman she did not know approached them. She could feel herself getting dizzy. He had a dazzling smile on his face, his longish hair was up in a bun with some loose curls spilling out. She put her hand in her pocket and pinched her thigh to bring her back to reality.

Arlene put her hand out. "Hi, I'm Arlene, I was told you were Steven, the man with a plan."

Steve shook her hand. "Steve, please. Welcome to our little shelter."

Liam looked around. "I'd say more than little. This place looks amazing."

"Steve, this is Liam Caffney." Arelene introduced him.

Steve shook Liam's hand. "It's very nice to meet you. And this is my top volunteer, Abigail. She's going to be guiding you through your day here with us."

"Ah cheers! Good deal. It's nice to meet you, Abigail." Liam looked over her face and body language to see if she was a fan. He didn't get any fan vibe off of her, it made him relax a bit. This could be a really fun day.

"Abi here came up with an idea we hope you are game for."

Liam smiled. "Try me."

"First we have a shirt for you to wear today." Abigail handed him his shirt.

"We actually have a lot of these shirts," Steve stated. "We were hoping you would be willing to sign some so we could use them to sell to raise even more money for the shelter today."

"I think I can handle that." Liam nodded.

Abigail looked at Steve and then back at Liam and Arlene. "We were also hoping you might be willing to do some personalizations on the shirts for a bit more money."

Arlene shook her head. "I don't know about that. He'll gladly sign a pile before we begin though."

Liam waved. "Hi, right here in the room. It's no problem, Leenie. If it raises more money, I say let's do it."

"Okay, but only for a limited time. Not the entire time he is here. Let's say an hour."

"Let's say two," Liam chimed in.

Abigail was doing her best not to get too excited. "Are you sure? I know we threw this on you last minute, it's perfectly fine to say no. Just you being here will raise more money than not."

"Oh, so you're a fan of the show?" Arlene asked.

Abigail shook her head. "I'm afraid not. I'm more of a reader. But I have quite a few students who are big fans."

"She's an English teacher at the local high school," Steve chimed in.

Abigail nodded. "I just started my honor seniors on Chaucer's *Canterbury Tales*."

Liam gave Arlene a look. "Really? Then we certainly have a lot to discuss. I just started reading it again. Haven't picked it up since university, but recently I felt the urge."

Abigail raised an eyebrow. "Of course. We can discuss it as you sign some shirts."

Liam laughed. "Ah, a real taskmaster I see. Well, lead the way!"

"Ah, shirts are in the storage room. Let me get them." Steve turned in the direction of the stock room.

"No worry, mate. I'm sure Abi here can lead the way. As long as there is a table I can sign away from there." He looked at Abigail. "You don't mind if I call you Abi, do you?"

"No, that's fine."

Liam put his arm out to her. "Thanks. Shall we?"

Abigail hesitated for a moment but then looped her arm in his and started for the storage room.

"Stop by the office and get some sharpies first!" Steve yelled after them.

Abigail put her thumb up in the air giving the okay sign.

Steve turned to Arlene. "Thank you again for this. We are really excited to have Liam here."

"It's our pleasure. I'm always happy to help my great uncle when he calls. This place was just a dream when I was a kid. It warms my heart to see how far his dream has come. And besides, Liam loves giving back to his fans, and he's a big animal lover, so it's perfect."

"Let me show you where he and Abi will be stationed." Steve led Arlene to the puppy pen in the front room.

# CHAPTER FOUR

A bigail pulled out a chair and handed Liam a couple of sharpie markers. "I'll grab you some shirts." She went to different boxes making sure she pulled out shirts in all sizes, tossing them at Liam as she pulled. One of the other volunteers walked in looking for Abigail.

"Hey Abi, do you know where the extra leashes—" Simone stopped mid-sentence. "Holy crap! You're Lochlan!"

Liam smiled but said nothing.

"Simone, this is Liam. Who is Lochlan?"

Liam stifled a laugh.

Simone pointed to Liam. "That's Lochlan, crown prince of Nyla in the realm of Everly. Oh my god! Can I have your autograph?!" Simone practically shrieked.

"Simone! Get a hold of yourself. We are not at a boy band concert!"

Liam laughed out loud. "Wow, I don't think I've ever been compared to a boy band before."

Simone's cheeks turned red. "Sorry. Um, I came in here for something."

"You mean something besides getting an autograph?" Liam winked at her. "Perhaps hoping to grab a photo?"

Abigail rolled her eyes. It was moments like this why she would never let him or anyone else she worked with know she was a fan. He was nice enough, but he was treating her very differently. It was subtle, but it was obvious enough to Abigail, although Simone seemed clueless. "I believe you were looking for the extra leashes.

"Abi, if you grab those extra leashes, I'll take a quick picture here with - I'm sorry, what's your name?"

"Um, Simone. I'm Simone. Really, I can take a picture with you?"

Liam nodded. "I'll even sign your shirt if you want."

All Simone could do was nod her head and smile.

Liam got up and walked over to Simone and held out his hand. "It's very nice to meet you, Simone. Thank you for watching the show. I'm so glad you like it."

Simone just kept nodding. "It's my favorite show on the air. I never miss an episode. Will you end up with Beatrice or are you going to marry Isla? Are you being renewed for another season?!"

"Sorry lass, I can't answer either of those questions. But promise me you'll keep watching to find out."

"Of course!" Simone smiled. She pulled out her phone to take a picture, and promptly dropped it on the floor.

Liam picked up her phone. "Allow me, darlin'. Smile pretty." Liam took the picture then handed the phone back to Simone. "Now, about that shirt."

"You can sign my chest if you like." She stuck out her chest for Liam.

"Simone!" Abigail admonished.

"I just meant the front!" Simone snapped back.

"How about I sign here on your sleeve?" Liam didn't wait for an answer, he signed the sleeve and went to sit back down.

Abigail handed a box of leashes to Simone. "Here you go, better get them out there." She turned Simone towards the door and gave her nudge to get moving. Once Simone was gone, Abigail turned towards Liam. "Sorry about that, but I have a feeling you are used to that."

Liam shook his head. "I don't know if I'll ever get truly used to that. However, I am very thankful for my fans. Without them, I have no series."

"Understandable, I guess. There's a chance she won't be the last staff member to treat you like that today, no matter what Steve may tell them. I'll do my best to keep them at bay."

Liam shrugged. "It comes with the territory. Thank you though."

"Sounds like you don't enjoy that part of the job."

Liam shrugged again. "You have to take the good with the bad."

"So you consider your fans bad?"

Liam's eyes grew wide as he vehemently shook his head. What was he doing? How could this woman he just met put him so at ease to let his guard down? What if she repeated what he said? It was easy enough to deny since only the two of them were in the room. He had to answer her. "Oh no! That's not what I meant at all. It's just complicated I guess."

Abigail knew she had put him on the spot. She needed to let him off the hook. "Well let's not complicate it for today. Let's just get some pets adopted." Abigail playfully threw another pile of shirts at Liam. "Follow me."

Abigail led him to the puppy pen. It was in a front room just off of the front doors. Steve had already set up the table and chairs for the two of them to sit at and for people to fill out adoption forms or get a shirt signed by Liam. The puppies clamored to the side of the pen with happy yaps aimed at Liam.

He chuckled at their cuteness. "They are adorable! Can I get in there with them?"

"Be my guest."

Liam climbed in and began to play with the puppies. He laughed and smiled as they licked at his face and jumped on and off his lap like he was their own personal pride rock. His happiness was contagious as he seemed off in his own little world, a world filled with puppy love. Abigail watched him for a moment. He had the look of pure joy on his face. She wondered how often he felt like that. She was pulled out of her thoughts by prospective pet owners beginning to come look at the puppies and then more to see the one and only Liam Gaffney up close and personal. They sold out of the pre-signed shirts within thirty minutes and were more than halfway through the personalized shirts by the time they hit the hour and a half mark.

"Can I get you a coffee or a hand massage?" Abigail asked jokingly.

"I'll take both please." Liam winked.

Arlene, who had been leaning on a corner wall reading a contract on her phone, called out to them. "I'll make a Starbucks run. I saw one down the street when we were driving in. Can I get you anything, Abi?" Arlene liked Abigail. She felt comfortable leaving Liam with her for a few moments.

Abigail gave Arlene a thankful smile. Although it had only been a couple of hours, it was the most jam packed adoption event she had been a part of. She was already tired with several hours to go and was desperate for a caffeinated drink. "I would love a venti iced cinnamon dolce latte, please and thank you."

"Coming right up." Arlene smiled. "And I already know what you want." She gave Liam's shoulder a squeeze as she left.

"She must really like you," Liam commented.

Feeling bold, Abigail grabbed his signing hand and began to massage it. She wasn't sure what had come over her, but instead of second guessing herself she just went with it. Her insides did a little flip at the warmth and softness of his hands. She wondered what they would feel like roaming freely across her body. At that very moment she was so happy to be black. He couldn't see her blush. "Why do you say that?"

Liam loved the way Abigail was massaging his hand. He could feel all the cramping from so many rapid-fire signings just start to melt away. She had such a delicate touch and to his surprise it made him tingle. So much so that he had to take a deep breath and concentrate on the question she had just asked him. "Leenie has been my agent since I started. She's like a big sister to me. She never, and I do mean never, leaves my side when I do events alone. Hence, she likes you. She clearly felt safe leaving me here with you and the puppies."

Abigail gave herself an internal high five. "How do you feel about kittens?"

"Kittens?"

"Yeah, you must need a break, and the kittens are a little further back, tends to be quieter."

"Your massage feels really good. My hand feels better already."

Abigail smiled. "I've been told I have magic fingers." *Who was this woman?* she wondered. She was never this bold.

"Oh really?" Liam raised an eyebrow.

Abigale quickly gave his hand one last pat and then let go. "Come on, let's say hi to the kittens." She walked him into the kitten room. She picked up a sweet little calico and handed it to Liam; it immediately crawled up his chest and curled up in the crook of his neck by his shoulder.

Abigail laughed. "You're stuck with her now, guess you'll have to adopt her."

Liam gently scratched the little kitten ball. "I guess I will."

Abigail was shocked. "I was only kidding. You don't actually have to adopt her."

"I could use the company. Do you have any?"

Abigail nodded. "Two cats, a brother and sister. I've had them since they were kittens. They are three years old now. I got them from here actually."

"Two? Really? What are their names?"

"Uh, yes. I was only going to get one, but then I didn't want her to be alone while I was at work, so I got her brother too."

"And their names?" Liam asked again.

Before she could answer, a group of girls came in asking for photos. Liam graciously took selfies with all of them. The cat never moved. It gave Abigail a moment to think, and she had to think fast. She couldn't tell him that her cats were named Lochlan and Beatrice. The stifled giggles and squeals told Abigail her time was up. She needed to give him an answer. She waited until the group filed out. "I named them Cassieopia and Dipper, after my two favorite constellations."

"Ah, you're a star gazer are you?"

Abigail smiled. "Among other things."

"I'd like to hear more about the other things."

Abigail was stunned. Was Liam flirting with her? And if so, was it a genuine flirt or a television personality flirt? And was there even a difference? She guessed there had to be a difference.

"Maybe we could have dinner together?" Liam interrupted her thoughts.

"Sure that would be very nice," Abigail squeaked out, her nerves betraying her voice.

Liam was a little surprised she said yes. He was even more surprised that he had been worried she might say no. "Can I pick you up at seven? That will give me time to freshen up and set up my new roommate here. Maybe you can help me figure out a name for her at dinner."

Abigail nodded. "Seven sounds great." She had found her voice again.

"What sounds great?" Arlene asked as she handed each of them an iced coffee. "I couldn't find you for a minute, but then I saw a crowd of young women coming back from this way and I figured it was a safe bet."

"Abi here has agreed to have dinner with me. And I've decided to adopt this little beauty here on my shoulder."

Arlene was quiet for a moment but quickly recovered. "I think that's a great idea. Well, the dinner, not sure about the cat. Um, Liam, can I talk to you privately for a moment?"

Arlene walked him over to a quiet corner in the room.

"What's up?" Liam asked as he tried to remove the calico from his shoulder. She just doubled down and began to purr so he left her there.

"Do you really think that dinner is a good idea?"

Liam shrugged. "I like Abi. She's great to be around. I can relax around her, it's really quite nice. Besides, it's just dinner, and I'm hoping she can answer some questions about *Canterbury Tales* for me."

"About that, I got a call today. The role is yours if you want it. I still need to iron out some things in your contract but it's all yours." Arlene smiled. "You just can't tell anyone yet."

Liam grabbed her into a hug lifting her off the ground for a moment. His six foot stature was no match for her small five foot four frame. "You are the best! But of course mums the word. I know better than to say anything."

"So your Chaucer conversation at dinner?"

Liam chuckled "Remember, this isn't my first rodeo. The conversation will be about the book and finding a name for this beauty on my shoulder. Speaking of, would you mind getting her on my flight with me? And maybe pick up a small litter box and some food? I'll gather the good stuff when I get home."

"You mean home to the city you are filming in and will be leaving in four months to go shoot somewhere else for two months?"

Liam's shoulders slumped. "But she's so cute."

"Look, I'll make the arrangements and pick up some things to last you until the flight if you really want me to, but you need to really think this through."

"I already told Abi I was taking her."

A big smile slowly crept across Arlene's face. "Well, well, well. I believe you are turning into a smitten kitten right before my eyes."

"Stop, Leenie."

"No, no, there is a glint in those eyes I haven't seen in a while. Did I mention that *Tales* is filming only an hour from this lovely little Connecticut town?"

Liam couldn't control his smile. "Leenie, can you help me out or not?"

"Of course. Do you know where you want to take her for dinner?"

Liam looked at her with a sweet smile and batted his eyes. "I have no idea. Maybe you could—"

"Boy! You're lucky I like you! I'll see what I can find." Arlene looked over at Abigail. She was helping a guest pick out the perfect kitten. It was obvious she was great with children.

"You do realize the two of you will be all over twitter and Instagram if you take her out tonight. I mean of course today's function will be, but dinner is an entirely different ballgame. Is she ready for that?"

Liam looked over at Abigail. It snuck up on him, but he realized he felt happy. Could it be that his heart was beginning to soften again after his very hurtful and very public breakup with his former co-star Bianca Monroe two years ago? He didn't want to think about that. Arlene didn't give him another minute to think about it.

"Hey, just do me a favor. Don't stay out too late. We both have early morning flights, and I promised the show you'd be ready for a short night shoot when you got back. No dialogue. Just that fight scene in the water you were rehearsing all last week."

Liam nodded and crossed his heart. "Scouts honor. Relax, it's just dinner. It's not like I'm asking her to marry me."

Arlene shook her head. She wasn't as sure of that as he was. "Okay, if you say so. I'll see what I can come up with."

"You really are the best!" Liam gave her a kiss on the cheek. "And I'm keeping the kitten." He walked back over to Abigail.

# CHAPTER FIVE

T he adoption day had been long but worth it. Liam's shirts alone raised almost two thousand dollars. And it had been one of their highest adoption rates to date. Abigail flopped on the couch smiling to herself thinking about Liam adopting that sweet little calico. She felt a little bit of guilt since she had suggested it, well implied it really. Forced him maybe? Abigail shook off the feeling. He could have said no at any time. She cuddled Lochlan and Beatrice as she thought about what she wanted to wear.

Abigail started laughing uncontrollably. She had a date, and not just any date, but a date with Liam Caffney. The sixteen year old fangirl deep inside her was doing the happy dance. The moment didn't last long as a sense of panic came over her. Her mind began to run a mile a minute on what could or couldn't happen. That it could be wonderful or a complete disaster, or worse, come off like one big joke. Abigail shook her head. No, she needed to get a grip. Everything was going to be fine. She headed to the shower to clear her head and figure out what she would wear.

She had no idea where they were going, and she didn't want to be overdressed or underdressed. She wanted something that showed off her curves but wasn't necessarily sexy, but she didn't want to be frumpy. She shook her head. None of her clothes were frumpy. Abigail was very meticulous about that. It was hard enough to find decent plus size clothes so when she found a good source, she allowed herself the indulgence of the exorbitant prices the store gouged her and other plus size beauties out of. It was extortion, plain and simple.

With one last rub to the ears for each of them, Abigail headed to her closet. Hands on hips she stared at her clothes, willing the perfect outfit to reveal itself. "By the Goddess of Nyla and all the realm, I need a great outfit!" Abigail sighed. But then like the magic of the fae, an outfit materialized in her mind. She flipped through the hangers looking for the blouse and pants she saw in her mind. Why hadn't she thought of it sooner? It would be perfect, she hoped.

Abigail took a deep breath and one last look in the mirror before she left her house. They were meeting at one of her favorite Italian Bistros. She was surprised he had chosen it since it was on a main strip downtown. This being a Saturday, it was sure to be busy. The thought made her stop in her tracks. Was this just a publicity opportunity for him? Taking the girl he volunteered with, out for a meal. Was she just more charity work for him? Abigail laughed as she slapped her cheek softly several times. She was letting her paranoia show through. This wasn't like her, losing her confidence. She chastised herself for the momentary lapse. This was nothing more than extending the interesting and fun time they had this afternoon. Nothing more and nothing less.

Arlene had arranged for them to meet at the restaurant, instead of having Liam pick her up. Liam swallowed hard and rubbed the sweat from his palms as he saw Abigail walk up. Her braids were down, unlike this afternoon when they were in a high ponytail. They fell around her face in a way that was captivating to him. He had only just arrived himself but wanted to wait outside for her. He gave her a hug as she reached the door. "You look wonderful."

Abigail looked down and smiled, happy with her outfit choice. She had decided on a pair of black slacks that had an intricate knot design in a very thin cream colored thread. It could be missed if the light didn't hit in just the right way. For the top she had settled on a cream deep scoop neck sleeveless top that showed off her cleavage nicely as well as the necklace her best friend Tess had given her on her last birthday.

It was the kind of shirt that hugged in all the right places, especially on a bigger frame, the kind of shirt that was so amazing, she had it in three other colors. Her shoes were a simple black ankle boot with a heel that was about half an inch. Heels were not a big thing for Abigail, especially in months when snow and ice were possible. These were both fashionable and super comfortable. "Thank you. You clean up pretty nice yourself."

Liam hadn't planned on having a nice dinner out while he was in town and Arlene had come to his rescue and picked him up a v-neck long sleeve shirt that had just a little heft to it to keep him warm, in a shade of green that made his eyes sparkle even more. Black pants were a staple in his wardrobe, so he had been safe there. He chuckled as he realized he too had black boots on. But his boots weren't ankle length, they would be considered calf length. Doc Martin's were his favorite, but no heel for him. "Before we go in, I just wanted to make sure that you are okay with getting your picture taken. I'm sorry, I should have asked earlier, but I can guarantee if you walk in there with me and have a meal with me your photo will be taken and displayed who knows where."

Abigail nodded. The thought had crossed her mind while she was getting ready at home. She knew it would be inevitable. But she also knew it would blow over quickly as this was a one time thing and there would be something bigger and better to gossip about by Monday. "It's fine, it's not like we'll be walking out of a hotel room or anything," she joked. "It's just dinner."

Laughing, Liam nodded. "That's pretty much what I told Leenie, but I just wanted to double check with you first." He opened the door to the restaurant. "Shall we?"

Abigail stepped in and up to the host stand. Liam moved up next to her and smiled at the young hostess who looked like she had just seen a ghost. "Hello there, you should have a reservation for two under the name Wheems."

The hostess nodded as she looked for the name, nodded as she crossed it off the list and grabbed two menus. "Just follow me please." She sat them at the table and handed Abigail her menu first. As she handed Liam his, she leaned in and whispered, "I love you on the show," then scurried away quickly.

Abigail watched her go, wondering why she was so quick with the compliment.

Liam waved his hand as if knowing her thought. "She would have gotten in trouble if her manager saw her do that. It's happened before."

Abigail smiled. "So it seems you're reading my mind now. Okay, swamy, what am I wondering now?"

Liam took her hand in his, closed his eyes and stroked her hand several times before speaking. "You are wondering why the reservation was under the last name Wheems. You're wondering if that is my real last name, or just the name I use when making reservations."

Abigail gently pulled her hand away. "Okay, now you're freaking me out."

Liam laughed. "Wheems is Leenie's last name."

"That's Arlene right? I thought I heard you call her Leenie today."

Liam nodded. "Yup, it's my nickname for her. It helps from keeping too many looky loos coming in or making reservations at the same time to catch a glimpse."

Abigail cocked her head, raising an eyebrow. "You have my sympathy?"

"I know, I know, first world problems. I do keep it in perspective though. I promise."

That answer seemed to satisfy Abigail. She sat back and started looking at the menu. The server came over and filled their water and then asked, "Can I get you any appetizers this evening?"

Liam looked at Abigail. She just shrugged. Liam took another look at the menu. "Can we get an order of stuffed mushrooms and an order of calamari please. Oh and a bottle of Vineyard West Petite Syrah."

The server nodded. "I'll put that right in for you and then come back with your drinks. My name is Matthew." He gave them both a nod and walked away.

Liam looked at Abigail. Her chocolate eyes had a richness to them, with just a swirl of gold, it was almost hypnotic to him. He blinked, realizing he had stared a moment too long. "I hope you don't mind what I ordered."

"Not at all! And that is actually one of my favorite wines. But how did you discover it? I'm assuming from that amazing accent, the U.S. is not your home."

"You think my accent is amazing, do you?" Liam winked.

Abigail was slightly flustered, but she recovered quickly. "You know the old saying, women are always suckers for accents."

"I wouldn't call you a sucker, but I'm glad you like my accent. But to answer your question I've lived in Manhattan for about six years now. So I found the wine somewhere along the way there. A lot of places carry it, which makes me happy."

"Shut up! I lived in Manhattan for undergrad and grad school. I moved up here when I got offered a teaching position."

"Didn't want to teach in the big bad city?"

"Ha! No, it was time for me to go. I wanted a little more nature and a little less concrete."

Liam nodded. "Understandable, to be honest with my work schedule, I've been there maybe a total of two years timewise with all the traveling I do with work."

"And you adopted a kitten?! Sorry, that didn't come out the way I meant it to."

Laughing, Liam put his hand over hers. He realized how much he liked the physical contact. He leaned in. "Now you sound just like Leenie. She's worried I won't have time for - you know I still don't have a name for her. Will you help me think of one?"

Liam was looking directly in her eyes now. Abigail felt her pulse begin to quicken a little and all of a sudden, her mouth became dry. She loved looking in his eyes. She still couldn't believe this was happening. But then she had to ask herself what was happening? The answer was nothing, it was just dinner. "Um, sure, sure."

Matthew came back with their wine, breaking the moment. He took their dinner order promising the appetizers shortly and left them alone again. Before they could resume their conversation a woman about Abigail's age came up to the table. "I'm so sorry to bother you. But I just had to tell you how much I enjoy watching you on *EverMorphs*. Would you mind signing an autograph for me?" She handed him a clean napkin she had grabbed off the empty table next to them.

Liam gave the woman one of his best smiles. "That's so kind of you to say. Of course I will, my darlin' what's your name?"

"My name is Monica." She looked Abigail up and down and gave her a little half smile. "Is this your girlfriend?"

Abigail was stunned at the audacity of this woman, this stranger, to ask someone she really didn't know such a personal question. But Liam seemed to take it in stride.

"Oh no! I've never been lucky enough to call this one my girl. She's a dear friend I've known since before I hit puberty. Maybe one day I'll be lucky enough to call her my gal." Liam blew Abigail a kiss and winked at her.

He didn't see the dirty look Monica gave Abigail as he was signing the napkin. To no one's surprise she had a sharpie in purse. Monica changed her tune as Liam was finishing up. "Thank you so much. I'll let you get back to your dinner. It was wonderful to meet you." Monica stroked and squeezed his shoulder as she walked away. She'd only taken two steps before she whipped out her phone and quickly took a picture. Liam and Abigail could see the flash out of the corner of their eyes.

"I cannot believe you said that! Did you see the dirty look she gave me?!"

Liam stifled a laugh. "I'm sorry Abi, I couldn't resist. I've met that woman so many times and given her photos and autographs up the wazoo. I really didn't think I would run into her here. And if she realized that I recognized her, she would have been here another twenty minutes taking a walk down memory lane."

"She sounds like a super fan. I know the event today was supposed to be advertised. Maybe she was there too. You know that photo is probably already up on her Instagram page."

"Or her twitter feed." Liam snickered.

"Ha ha sir! Very funny." Abigail shook her head.

The waiter brought over their food and refilled their wine glasses before departing again.

"So, the way you said super fan. Sounded like there was some disdain in your voice."

Abigail took a large sip of her wine. "Not really, it was just an observation."

"An observation you didn't like." Liam was pushing.

"I just am not a fan of being a *fan* of anything really. Let alone a *super fan*."

"Super fan was your word, not mine."

Abigail was uncomfortable with the conversation, and she really didn't want to get into her issues with being a fan with the likes of Liam Caffney. "Can we change the subject please? We really need to find a name for your kitten."

"I'm sorry if I upset you. Of course a name is definitely in order." Liam knew there was something more there, but this wasn't the time or place to push. And he genuinely hoped there would be another time.

"Maybe you should give her an Irish name. Something to remind you of home."

Liam smiled. "That's a really good idea. It has been too long since I have been able to make a trip home."

"Maybe you can go after *EverMorphs* finishes filming. Arlene mentioned you were still filming?"

Liam nodded. "I would, but I might have another project that would start too soon for me to go back home. Maybe after that and before the next season of *EverMorphs* starts up again."

"Sounds like you never have much down time."

"No, I don't. But gotta keep busy while the public still wants to see my face. I'm thankful for the work."

"You're really quite talented."

"Ah-ha! So you have seen *EverMorphs*!" Liam smiled. He was only teasing but he liked the idea that she had seen the show at least once. Even if she might not have liked it.

Abigail shook her head. "Sorry to disappoint you, but I actually saw you in a movie. I can't remember the name, but it was filmed in black and white and you played a pianist who was losing his sight. You were brilliant, I cried." Abigail took another sip of wine. She couldn't believe how much lying she was doing. Was it really lying or more of an omission? She remembered the name of the movie, it was called *Keys,* she owned the blu-ray version of it! The worst part was she actually liked Liam. Not that she thought she would ever see him again, but still.

"I think I'm going to go with Aoife. It means beautiful, like you." Liam took a drink. He hadn't expected to say that. It kind of just slipped out. He really hoped she didn't think he was being phony with her like he had been with Monica.

"I think that's a lovely name. I'm sure you'll be very happy with her, and she will give you lots of love."

"So tell me Abi, when you are not working at the shelter or teaching English, what do you like to do?"

"Well, I really like to write. Sometimes poems, but mostly fiction."

"Short stories or novels? Have you ever tried to publish anything?" Liam was intrigued.

"Oh no, I just do it for myself. Once upon a time I thought of being an author, it just wasn't meant to be. But I love teaching, and I still have time to write. Even if I'm the only one who reads it."

"Well I'd love to read something you wrote. I love to read."

"Really? What are you reading now?"

"Oddly enough, *The Canterbury Tales.*"

Abigail tried to keep her wine in as she laughed out loud. "Are you serious? You're just saying that!"

"No, no, it's true. I picked it up and was reading it on the plane. It's sitting on the night table in my hotel room right now. If I'm honest I'm actually having a bit of trouble with it."

"I'd be happy to help you with it if you want. It's kinda what I do." Abigail smiled. Helping him meant continuing some kind of relationship with him. She wanted that more than anything at this very moment.

Liam reached across and squeezed her hand. "That would be wonderful. I'd really like that."

Abigail squeezed his hand back and nodded. She wanted to solidify a tutoring schedule with him, but now was not the time. She wasn't in teacher mode, she was in date mode. "Okay, so when you aren't acting, or reading, or cuddling your brand new kitten, what do you like to do? What would you be if you weren't an actor?"

Liam leaned back in his chair. "Oh, such a loaded question. Shall we discuss it over dessert?" Liam waved the waiter over. He ordered Tiramisu for both of them along with some tea. "Oh, I'm sorry, I did it again. I ordered for both of us. I hope that's okay."

"Well, I did order my own choice for the main dish. And your other choices were wonderful, so I think it's cute that you ordered for both of us. As a long time friend, I have to say you really know how to treat a lady." Abigail winked at him. They both began to laugh. "But seriously, you aren't an actor, what are you? Go!" Abigail just looked at Liam and twirled her wine glass.

"I guess I would say a photographer. I've been into photography since I was young. My aunt got me a camera for my twelfth birthday. At least I think it was my twelfth birthday. Anyway I've been taking pictures ever since. I've even framed a couple of them over the years, given some as gifts."

"I have a proposition for you." Abigail smiled.

Liam leaned and smiled. He almost reached for her hand again but fought the urge. "Oh really?"

"I'll show you mine if you show me yours." Abigail regretted it almost the second it came out of her mouth. It was such a loaded statement, and she didn't mean it the way it sounded. I mean she would love to see him—no! She needed to stop thinking like that. He was too good at reading her thoughts. He was very good with context clues.

"Why Abi, you little minx!"

"I meant I'll show you something I wrote if you share some of your photography."

"I know what you meant. I just like teasing you." Liam winked. "I would be honored to read some of your work. And I'll gladly share some of my photography. Just be kind please."

"Same to you."

They finished their dessert as they discussed places they had traveled, favorite books they had read, and the toughest game of sudoku they had ever played. The evening ended far too soon for the both of them. Liam paid, leaving Matthew a very generous tip. He opened the door for Abigail, being a true gentleman. "May I walk you to your car?"

"Of course. Thank you."

Liam clasped his hand in hers as they walked. Such a simple act made him giddy. It warmed him in a way that he hadn't felt in a long time. Abigail squeezed his hand. She didn't know how to even process her feelings at this moment, so instead she decided to just relish in the moment, to enjoy the feeling of Liam's warm hand in hers. The feeling of his pulse next to hers. She started to walk slower to prolong the feeling. In too few steps, they were standing at her car.

Liam decided not to think and just act. He turned Abigail to him and wrapped his arms around her waist letting them rest gently on her ass. He wanted to caress it but stopped himself. "Abi, can I ask you a question?"

"Of course," Abigail barely whispered.

"May I kiss you? I feel, I honestly feel, I don't know what I feel. I just know I will regret it if I—"

Not letting him finish his sentence, Abigail reached up and kissed him. She let her lips melt into his as he tightened his grasp on her. He caressed her ass as he deepened his kiss, and she opened her mouth to him. She ran her hands along his back and up to his neck, playing with his curls. They were lost in the moment of time, not aware of their surroundings anymore. Hearts beating fast, Liam finally began to pull back, remembering they were out in public. He quickly looked around. He didn't see anyone. If someone had been there before he wouldn't have noticed.

Abigail stepped back. Was he regretting the kiss, she wondered. Was it too public? She fumbled around in her purse for her keys. Liam grabbed her hand.

"Hey, are you okay? Did I overstep?"

"Are you embarrassed that you kissed me? Do you regret it?"

"God no! Why would you say that?"

"Because you're looking around like you don't want to be seen with me all of a sudden."

Liam pulled Abigail into a hug. "No, it's not that. I was just checking to see if anybody had taken a photo. I don't regret kissing you, please believe that. But this first kiss, this first amazing kiss, which I hope will only be the beginning, I want *that* kiss to have been just for us."

Abigail really didn't know what to make of all of this. But she did believe him. She just had no idea what this could all mean for the two of them.

# CHAPTER SIX

—◆————————◆—

A bigail was in a world of her own recounting every moment of the last several hours. She jumped out of her skin and screamed with mace in hand when the living room light went on as she was locking the front door behind her.

"Lucy! You gotta lot of esplaning to do!" yelled her best friend Tess in the worst Ricky Ricardo accent possible.

"Dammit Tess! I almost maced you! What are you doing here!"

"Well, you didn't answer your phone and I had to know exactly what the hell this is all about!" Tess showed her a picture on her phone. It was one of the many fan pages for *EverMorphs* and there, front and center, was a picture of her and Liam in the restaurant laughing over something. "I don't know what stuns me more, the fact that you went to dinner with the one and only Liam Caffney or that you didn't tell your best friend in the entire world that it was happening!"

"God! I never should have given you a key. That's supposed to be for emergencies."

"My best friend going on a date with Liam Caffney *is* an emergency."

Abigail put her purse down on the side table and flung her boots off her feet. She headed to the kitchen for some water. "I was going to call you the minute I got home. Would you like some tea?"

"Tea?" Tess followed her into the kitchen. "Got anything stronger?"

Abigail shook her head. "If I drink any more tonight, I won't be able to drink at brunch tomorrow. I had a lot of wine tonight." She poured them both a glass of water. "In fact, if we could table this discussion until tomorrow that would be great. I'm beat." Abigail gave her friend a hug and headed to her bedroom, closing the door behind her.

Tess promptly opened it. "Nope, you're not getting off that easy. We can skip brunch if you are too tired, but you are telling me everything that happened, and you are telling me now."

Abigail sighed. "Fine, can I just put my pajamas on first please?"

Tess whipped out an overnight bag she had lying by the coffee table. "Ha! A sleepover! You fell right into my trap. Go change, I'll change out here and make some popcorn.

Abigail splashed some cold water on her face and changed into her favorite pair of yellow striped jammy bottoms with a yellow sleep tank. She put her braids back in a loose ponytail so they wouldn't be flying around in her face. She smiled remembering how Liam had gently moved them out of her face when they were talking by her car. He had moved them again when he had kissed her goodnight in the car. She had offered to drive him back to the hotel so he wouldn't need to call Arlene or an Uber, he readily agreed. It was really just an excuse for a few more minutes together and they both knew it.

"Hey! Are you okay in there?" Tess knocked loudly on the door.

Abigail put a smile on her face and headed out to the living room. She wasn't sure just how much she wanted to share at the moment. Tess had set out popcorn and two cups of mint-lavender tea. She wrapped Abigail in a great big hug. That was all Abigail needed, she started to cry.

"Oh Abi! Don't cry. What's wrong? I thought you would be on cloud nine right now."

"I don't know why I'm crying. It was a great night really, he kissed me! And I really really liked it!" Abigail cried.

"Honey, you're not making any sense." Tess handed her some tea.

Abigail went on to explain everything that happened from the time Liam arrived at the shelter until she walked into her apartment to find Tess waiting there. The entire time Tess listened, giving Abigail her full attention and eating popcorn like she was watching a *Lifetime* movie.

"Holy shit, Abi. Like seriously holy shit!"

"I know, I know. But what do I do now? Maybe I do nothing. I mean it's not like he asked for my number."

"Alright, let's look at this logically. Liam doesn't live in this state. He travels for work all the time and is gone months and months at a stretch. What tonight was should be chalked up to just a beautiful moment in time. Don't try to think ahead or about the future. Especially since he doesn't even know what you are."

"You make me sound inhuman with your *'he doesn't know what you are'* talk."

Tess laughed. "I was just talking about the 'F' word. He doesn't know you are one."

"I think it would change everything if he did." Abigail hung her head. "I hate this! I never should have agreed to be his handler during the pet event. If I had just kept my distance, none of this would have happened."

"But it did. So as I see it, you have a couple of choices. One, come clean that you are a fan of his and a fan of the show."

Abigail made a face. "I don't like that option. You know how I feel about that word. It's just as bad as a four letter swear word. It leaves a bad vibe in the air and people treat you differently once it comes out of your mouth. What else do you have?"

Tess took a sip of tea. "You could just go with the flow and see what happens. Pray the truth will never come out."

"But the truth always comes out, doesn't it?" Abigail sighed.

Tess nodded. "Yes, yes it most certainly does."

Abigail shook off the feeling of dread. "Tess, I don't even know why we are discussing this. It's a moot point. It's like you said. He's not even from here. It was a glorious moment in time that I will have to cherish for the rest of my life."

"But you told me he asked for your help with Chaucer. That means there will be more contact."

Abigail shrugged. "For all I know he was just being nice. If he meant it, he would have asked for my phone number or at the very least my email address. That didn't happen, end of story."

Tess looked at her bestie. She wasn't sure if she believed her. Her gut told her there was more of this story that would play out. She just wasn't sure if it would be a good ending or a bad one.

# CHAPTER SEVEN

In Arlene's mind, Liam was being extra quiet on the plane ride back to Toronto. He just stared out the window, with Aoife safely stowed under his seat. She sighed remembering the days when more television shows were shot in New York, now almost everything seemed to be filmed in Toronto. She spent more time going back and forth because of her clients than she would have liked, but her personal touch was one of the reasons she was so successful. She tapped Liam on the shoulder. "Penny for your thoughts."

"I'm just a little tired, Leenie."

"Do you want to talk about it?"

Liam turned to Arlene. "You think I have something to talk about?"

"I think you need to talk about your date. I mean, it was a date, right?"

Liam couldn't keep the giant smile from crossing his face. "And a glorious one at that."

"So, what's the problem?"

"Well, for one, she's a civilian. The thought of throwing her into the spotlight, I don't know if that's fair to her."

Arlene snorted. "Trust me when I say she can hold her own. So that doesn't count. What else have you got?"

"I don't live anywhere near her?"

"Technically you only live one state, one train ride away."

"And I'm never home."

"Okay, you got me there. But listen Liam, in the short time I saw you with her, and make no mistake I had eagle eyes on you the whole time, your entire demeanor changed in a way I haven't seen in a very long time. It's worth investigating."

"Maybe?"

"She got you to get a kitten for Christ sake! I think it's worth a moment of your time to see what it could be."

Liam put his arm around Arlene giving her a side hug. "Leenie, you are the big sister I never wanted." He kissed her cheek. "Thank you."

"Well, I have some news that will make things a little easier for you, I hope. I have a wonderful contract for you to sign, and then it will be official. You will officially be the Pardoner on *Hidden Tales.*"

Liam leaned back in his seat and smiled. "Thank you, Leenie. You're the best." He closed his eyes and began to relax.

"Should I tell you I looked into Abi's background? You know, just in case."

Liam shot up in his seat. Eyes wide open. "You did what?!"

"Don't be mad. I was just being careful. Besides, I didn't find anything terrible. She has a private Instagram page, no Facebook or Twitter to speak of, and her LinkedIn is all about her teaching."

"I don't want to hear any more about this. You shouldn't have done that."

Arlene held her hands up. "Okay, okay. I won't mention it again."

Liam looked at Arlene. "Nothing terrible? But you did find something."

Arlene opened her mouth to speak but Liam shut her down.

"Nope!" Liam leaned back again and put his earbuds in. He was done talking for the duration of the flight.

# CHAPTER EIGHT

◆––––––––◆

*And That's All I Have To Say About That!*

*All Things EverMorph All the Time*

S*eason 4 Episode Highlights - the BIG reveal of who was spying on Lochlan and Beatrice! Lowlight - Where the hell is Flint!!!*

*Greetings Everrites and Morphlings. WOW! Just WOW!! This week's episode was in one word, AMAZING. Try to tell me differently! Go ahead! Try! You can't, can you? I knew it!! Alright let us bask in the awe and wisdom of the episode for a moment. For all of you who thought it was Nyx spying, you are the big winners. But did you see what she turned into? Am I the only one who didn't know that maiden fairies could transform into warrior elfkins!? What kind of weird hybrid breeding makes that possible? I need* some serious backstory on that one please! I mean she freaking bit Lochlan! If Beatrice hadn't hit her from behind, I really think she would have bit that arm clean off! Thank the Goddess Beatrice has all that medical training (wink wink).

BUT where the hell was Flint? Isn't he supposed to be Locahlan's right hand man, best friend, and most importantly HIS PROTECTOR?!? Yes, yes, they were having a relatively private moment, but Flint should be within earshot. ESPECIALLY if Lochlan is venturing into the human world! He better have been kidnapped by Oberon, or being seduced by Zarina. I think those are the only two reasons I will accept at this moment. What about you? Come on Fae folk, share your thoughts and comments.

Until next time EternallyEvers OUT!!

Comments: **NyxIsMySpiritGuide:** Hell yeah Nyx was spying! I'm hoping her actions will show Isla how much she really loves her.

Response: **NylaKingdom4Ever** Sorry but Isla will never leave Lochlan. She loves him. Even with his actions of late.

**RogansRaiders:** That transformation was awesome! I'm with you EE I want some serious back story on that!

**Morphing4Oberon:** Something bad is definitely happening with Flint. He would NEVER leave Lochlan unprotected.

**LochlanIsMine:** Lochlan will find Flint, I mean once he's done flirting with Beatrice. LOL

\* \* \*

"Miss Reese!" Jacob raised his hand urgently.

"Yes, Jacob?" Abigail asked as she wrote some of her famous 'think for a moment' questions on the board about the reading from the weekend homework assigned. Abigail usually wasn't one of those teachers who regularly assigned weekend homework. She wanted her students to have their weekends free to pursue hobbies and other interests like she did. But the past weekend had required a little reading because her students just weren't picking up Chaucer as easily or as quickly as she had hoped.

"This assignment. I got so frustrated. I had to stop and start at least ten times. There has got to be an easier way." A wave of murmurs of agreement swept across the room.

Abigail turned to her students. "Okay, alright, time for a ring of truth." She went to her filing cabinet and pulled out a bag of tootsie pops. "Everyone, shoes off and take a seat on top of the desks." She placed one Tootsie pop on every desk and then went to the middle of the figure eight. "You all are intelligent human beings and because I respect you, I do not want to dumb down Chaucer for you. I want you to be challenged, even pushed a little. But I don't want it to get so frustrating for you that you completely give up. So, we are going to try a couple of different things. But before we do any of that do any of you have any questions I could help you with right now?"

Several hands shot up in the air. Abigail sighed a little internally. Her head exploding sticker was coming to fruition way too soon in the segment. Abigail pointed to Amanda. "Yes Amanda?"

"Did you go on a date with Liam Caffney this past weekend?"

"Shut up," Margot shrieked "For real?"

Amanda nodded "Yes! See?" Amanda pulled a fan page for *EverMorphs* on Instagram and handed her phone to Margot. She swooned over the photos and then handed the phone to Rebecca who also swooned and handed it off to someone else.

"No phones in my class, Amanda! You know the rules."

"Wait, is he the dude from the TV show with all the fairies? My sister loves that crap." Keith laughed as his turn to view the pictures came around.

"Forget your little sister, I love that show and Lochlan is my favorite!" Amy exclaimed.

"He did that action movie with Ross Gander! I read he did all his own stunts. Well the ones the studio would allow him to do anyway," Robbie chimed in.

"He is so hot! I love him on *The EverMorphs*! Are you two like an item now? You know, he hasn't dated since what's her name broke up with him on the red carpet two years ago," Rebecca asked. The phone had now come full circle.

Abigail could see and hear that she had clearly lost the room. Hopefully she could get the room back on track. "Alright! Alright! Rebecca, please give Amanda her phone back. And Amanda, if I see your phone out again, I'm taking it and you won't get it back until your parents come see me to get it."

Amanda reached for her phone that Rebecca was handing to her. "Sorry Miss Reese. But are you? I mean did you?"

Abigail sighed. There was no way around this and Liam had warned her. "Let's just get this out of the way. Yes, Liam Caffeny and I had dinner last Saturday. He is a lovely person who helped do a fundraiser for the animal shelter I volunteer at. He was thanking me for helping him out. I was his chaperone for the event. And that is all there was to it." She tried not to recall their kiss as she told her students it was just dinner. "Now, there were some pictures taken at dinner and that is all you are seeing there. Just a thank you dinner. Now, we really need to get back to *Canterbury Tales*. Everyone please take out your copy and—"

Abigail's room intercom buzzed. She removed herself from the middle of the figure eight and picked up the room phone. "Yes."

"Miss Reese, will you please come to the office when you have a moment. There is a package down here for you," Estelle, the school secretary, spoke to her.

"Thank you. Can I send a student for it?"

Estelle laughed into the phone. "I don't really think you want your students picking this up for you."

"I'll be down in just a moment, thank you, Estelle." Abigail hung up the phone and turned back to the class. "Okay, I have to run down to the office for a moment. The drama scripts may have arrived. What I want you to do while I am gone is look at the table of contents in *The Canterbury Tales*. Without doing any research or looking up any of the character descriptions, look at the names of each story and write down the name of one that you think will interest you, just by the title alone." She turned to Margot. "Margot, please collect everyone's answers and put them in the 'pick me' jar and I'll be right back." Abigail closed her classroom door behind her, and she immediately heard loud voices coming from her room discussing the now infamous non-date date. She opened the door and popped her head in. "Hey! I expect better from you!" The class immediately quieted down, and she closed the door and headed down to the office.

Estelle was behind her desk typing when Abigail walked in. She did a quick scan of the counter for her package. She didn't see it. Estelle saw her, but she didn't stop typing, she just motioned with her head to the left. Abigail looked in that direction to find Steve smiling with a very odd sized box in his hands and some flowers on top of the box.

"Hey Abi, this was dropped off at the shelter for you today." Steve smiled. "It came by special courier. I didn't think it could wait until you came in again."

Abigail's eyes lit up. She didn't even have to see the label to know it was from Liam. She had no clue what he had sent but she could see that he sent something. She returned to Estelle. "Hey Estelle, can I leave these flowers with you until I go home? Bringing them up to my classroom will only incur a boat load of questions."

Estelle smiled and nodded. "You mean like who are the flowers from? Or do I even need to ask?"

Abigail shook her head and laughed. "Instagram?"

"Twitter," Estelle replied.

Abigail took the box from Steve. "Thanks for bringing this by."

"Are you going to open it?" Steve wanted to know what Liam had sent.

"I think I'll wait until I get home. I'm just going to run this to my car." Abigail turned to Steve. "Steve, I'll walk you out."

"Bell rings in fifteen." Estelle reminded her.

"Shit! Okay, I'll take this with me, and I'll be back for the flowers at the end of the day. Thanks a million, Estelle. I owe you one." She gave Steve a hug. "Thanks again Steve, I really appreciate you dropping this by. I'll call you later and tell you what's inside." She winked. "Maybe." She walked Steve as far at the front hall then turned left to head back up to her class.

To her students' credit, they were sitting quietly. Some had their Chaucer books open, others were on their phones. She only needed one guess as to what they were looking up. They quickly squirreled them away then they heard the doorknob. Abigail put the box down behind her desk. "Okay, Margot, let's have that 'pick me' jar." She took the votes out of the jar and counted them twice. "Alright, it looks like we are going to be working on The Pardoner's Tale first. So for now we will be setting aside the syllabus I so painstakingly made. "

The class gave her a collective "Aw".

Abigail chose to ignore it. "Tonight I want you to read the first three stanzas. Then write down what you think each stanza is trying to say. Don't overthink it, just follow the rhythm, the cadence of the piece. Use any context clues you read and most importantly go with your gut. We'll discuss your answers tomorrow." Abigail finished just as the bell rang. The class gathered their things and left.

The rest of the day, Abigail started each of her classes with 'the Liam question and answer session'. She was glad when the day was finally over. She grabbed her things including her box from Liam before heading down to the office to grab her flowers.

"They really are quite lovely. I got several compliments on them today," Estelle mentioned.

"Thanks for keeping them safe for me. Estelle, I really appreciate it." Abigail smiled as she smelled them.

"That must have been some amazing dinner to garnish such a lovely bouquet." Estelle whistled.

Abigail hadn't taken a good look at it before but now that she had time, she could see how elaborate it was. It was full of vibrantly colored flowers and it was a bit of an eclectic bunch. There were roses, peonies, lavender, sunflowers, lilacs, daffodils, and lilies of the valley. She wasn't even sure if all the flowers were in season at the moment. They hadn't discussed flowers, so he had no idea what her favorites were, but he had managed to get a few of them in there. "It was a lovely dinner." Abigail smiled. "See you tomorrow, Estelle. Thanks again!"

Abigail knew Estelle wanted more details, but Tess was the only person she had any intention of sharing details about Liam and her night with him.

# CHAPTER NINE

A bigail arrived home and put her things down. She went to change into something more comfortable. She always dressed in style for work, taking great pride in making sure she looked good. But she also loved a good pair of yoga pants and an oversized tee shirt. She headed to the kitchen to see what she wanted to do for dinner. As she stared at her open fridge she sighed, nothing looked appetizing enough to her. She grabbed her phone and ordered food from her favorite Indian food restaurant.

She sat on her couch and turned on the DTV channel. Design Television was her favorite station. She loved any kind of home improvement, house flipping, home building type of shows. By this same time next year, Abigail knew she would be ready to start the hunt for a home. Her apartment living days were coming to an end and she couldn't have been more happy. Feeling relaxed, she finally began to open the box.

Abigail was stunned as she opened the box and peeled away the layers of bubble wrap and tissue. Inside were three framed photos. One was of a sunset over the water, the colors were just brilliant. There was also one of a four leaf clover. It was a close up that looked like it had been captured in the early morning, as there was a drop of dew ready to fall off one of the four leaves. Abigail was amazed thinking what he had to do to get that shot. The last photo was a black and white of Liam. The light and shadow made him look almost ethereal. She didn't even have to ask but she knew he had used a timer and taken the picture himself. There was something so raw and sensual about it, she doubted any photographer would have been able to pull that kind of look out of him. It was a quiet moment between him, his soul and the camera. She was honored and humbled that he had shared such an intimate picture. In the bottom of the box was a card.

Abigail read, *'I showed you mine, when can I see yours ;) I'd call you, but I don't have your number. So here is mine. Hope to hear from you - Liam 917- 555- 3663'.* Abigail felt giddy. She wanted to call him immediately but for a brief moment wondered if it would make her look desperate. She laughed before she could even finish the thought. This man had gotten on a plane back to Toronto and within forty-eight hours had gotten these photos together and the flowers as well and made sure they had found their way to Abigail.

Abigail looked at the address on the return label. It was a Canadian address with Arlene's name. It made sense to her that Liam had put Arlene's address on it. Hell, maybe Arlene had mailed it for him. Regardless, she now had an address to 'show him hers' with. Getting off her couch she headed for her closet in her bedroom. The best thing about this apartment besides the amazing balcony was the extra large master closet. Abigail was able to fit a two drawer filing cabinet in the closet and it still left plenty of room for all her other belongings and other bits and baubles she kept in there.

Abigail was old school in many ways. She wrote all her stories and poems with pen and paper before ever dancing her fingers across a keyboard to memorialize her words in a computer file. She wanted to find the perfect story and poem to send to Liam. Something that matched the intimacy of what he had shared with her. Abigail made herself comfortable on the floor as she opened the first drawer. She was really proud of some of her earlier pieces but knew she had progressed as a writer and had really hit her stride with some of her later work. After two hours of searching that had also included a quick dinner break she had settled on one poem and two short stories.

Once picked, she went to her computer and printed out fresh copies, each on different color paper. She carefully used her three hole punch and then bound each one separately with different colored thick ribbons. For the poem she glued a dried flower, a daisy, since the poem was kind of about a daisy. It hung above the title like an umbrella sheltering the poem from the rain. Once they were wrapped in tissue and placed in a box she wrote a quick note to Liam, sealed the box and addressed it in care of Arlene.

Abigail picked up her phone to call the number. Her mouth got really dry. She went to the kitchen and got a glass of water. She downed that and then poured herself a glass of wine. The same kind she had with Liam at dinner. She let her mind wander back to the dinner and was only drawn out by the click of her phone call being connected. Liam picked up on the second ring.

"Hello?"

"Do you always pick up your phone so quickly?" Abigail smiled into the phone.

"Abi! I was hoping it was you."

She was pleased he remembered her voice so well. "Thank you so much for the photos. They are truly beautiful. And the flowers were as well. They made quite a statement."

"Oh really? What kind of statement?" Liam smiled through the phone.

Abigail got comfortable on the couch, drawing a blanket over her. "Steve dropped them off at my school."

"Ah! Sorry about that. Leenie only knew the address to the shelter."

"Oh don't be! Steve was in all his glory bringing me the box and flowers. He's very invested in the intrigue of it all." Abigail laughed. "And so were my students."

"Oh, no, dare I ask what happened?"

"Just what you mentioned. Photos of us at the restaurant. My students were all over it like white on rice."

"Haha! Sorry, I know I shouldn't laugh." Liam tried to stifle himself.

"No, go ahead, laugh. It was quite comical. I should have expected it. You have quite a few fans among my students."

"Good to know, good to know."

There was something in his voice that concerned Abigail, but she couldn't put her finger on it. "I didn't tell them anything if that's what you are concerned about."

"Oh no, I know you wouldn't say anything. I mean if you want to tell them how much I enjoyed kissing you, that's up to you but—"

"Oh no! TMI. I'm their teacher." Abigail laughed. "But you're right. I did enjoy kissing you."

"Mmm, it was lovely, wasn't it? Such soft lips you have. And you smell so good. I can't wait to see you again." Liam chuckled, trying to make light of what had just involuntarily slipped out of his mouth. "But anyway, I like that I'm bringing some intrigue into your life. Only time will tell what else I can bring to it."

"I look forward to it."

"So do I. What's that I hear in the background?"

"You can hear that?"

"Aye, I've been told I have bat-like hearing."

Abigail couldn't help but laugh. "Me too! My best friend Tess is always telling me that."

"So, what are you watching?"

"I'm watching Design Do-overs on—"

"DTV! I love that channel!! Can't do home improvement to save my life but I love watching all kinds of shows about it!"

Talking with Liam was so easy. There were no awkward pauses. They talked for two hours about everything and nothing at all. Abigail was laughing more in those two hours than she had in the last two months.

"So?" Liam asked with a little mischief in his voice.

"So what?" Abigail asked.

"When can I see yours?"

"You should see mine in a few days. It's all packed, I'm taking it to FastWay Express tomorrow."

"And then we can discuss my thoughts about it in person."

Abigail sat straight up. Her blanket falling down to her feet. "What do you mean?"

"I have a weekend off in a little less than two months. I could always come down."

"You'd come all the way down from Toronto. Just to see me?"

"I want to see you again, Abi. Don't you want to see me?"

"More than anything!" Abi gushed, and then she was silent. She prayed she didn't sound too eager. It had been a while since she had done this whole flirting, possible relationship thing. She felt like a big ol' fish out of water.

"Abi? Abs? Are you still there?"

"I'm here, I just—"

"So I'll see you in two months?"

"Yes, absolutely."

"I can hear your smile, you know," Liam practically cooed into the phone.

"Right back at you," Abigail responded.

"Maybe pick out a restaurant too? I'd like to take you to your favorite place."

Abigail held her breath for a moment and then let it out. "How about if I cook for you instead?"

"I would love that."

"Now who's smiling into the phone.?" Abigail laughed.

"I hate to end this lovely conversation, but I have an early call tomorrow." Liam yawned.

"Me too. I have to convince my kids that Chaucer is really awesome to read."

"Sounds like we both have big days tomorrow. Goodnight. I hope you sleep well."

"I will. Goodnight."

Three days later Arlene called Liam. "I have what appears to be a lovely package for you."

Liam laughed. "You get a lot of lovely packages for me Leenie, why call me about this one?

"Because this one happens to be from one Miss Abigail Reese. I can always put it in your pick up pile for the end of the month if—"

"Don't you dare!" Liam practically screamed as he almost jumped out of the makeup chair.

Rhonda, the makeup artist working on him, gave him a stern look. He mouthed 'sorry' as he sat back down.

"Can you bring it to the studio? If not, I'll swing by on my lunch break. It'll be a dash, but I can make it."

Arlene loved how excited he sounded about the package from Abigail. "I know you've been waiting for this. I won't torture you and make you wait. I'll bring it to your trailer in about an hour.

"You really are the best." Liam smiled.

An hour later Arlene drove onto the lot and headed to Liam's trailer. As she was walking, she slowed and then stopped dead in her tracks. She took a long look and was shocked to see Bianca Monroe talking to Andie the showrunner. Arlene couldn't fathom why she was talking to Bianca, but she knew it couldn't be good, at least not for Liam. The last thing Liam needed right now was that kind of poison walking back into his life.

Arlene made a mental note to find out what was going on. She needed to know if she needed to go into warrior mode for Liam. She wasn't joking when she said he was her favorite client. She would always go to bat for him, and bring out the barracuda fangs if she needed to. Shaking the feeling off, she put it out of her mind for the moment. She had a happier reason for being at the studio. She continued on her way to Liam's trailer. She knocked on the door, but didn't wait for an answer before entering.

"Special delivery," Arlene said in her sing-song voice. She looked around, but Liam wasn't there. She left the box on the dining table, by the couch. She scrounged around for a piece of paper and wrote *don't forget to tell me what's inside!* and left it next to the package. Making sure she had closed the door tightly behind her, Arlene headed back to her car.

Liam wasn't able to get back to his trailer until lunch. He practically sprinted back to his trailer. Sitting down, he carefully opened the box and read the note Abi had left him. He sat back on the couch and smiled as he read it. He wished she was here in Canada with him. There was so much more he wanted to learn about her.

He grabbed a bottle of water from his mini-fridge before opening anything else. Making himself comfortable he moved the tissue paper aside and pulled out the poem. Touching the daisy he made a mental note that Abigail was crafty, and from reading the poem, she had a strong pull to and respect for nature. He traced the flower one last time before setting it aside to read the next piece.

Liam loved the ingenuity of the ribbon closure and wondered if she had a craft drawer somewhere in her apartment. He'd have to take a look when he went to see her. His heart skipped a beat at the thought of seeing Abigail again, touching her, hearing her laugh, curling a braid between his fingers. Liam pulled himself out of his thoughts so he could read the first short story. From the second sentence he was enveloped in her words, in the world she had created. By the end he was wiping away a few tears. He put it down and took a big swig of water. He wanted to read the other one, but he needed to grab some food and meditate before he returned to set. He put the story and the poem back in the box and sent a quick text to Abigail and then headed out to get some lunch.

* * *

"Hello?"

"Hello my lovely."

Abigail smiled as she snuggled down on the couch under her favorite blanket. Liam had called earlier than expected. "You're done early tonight."

"Aye, the director had to cut the day short due to a location glitch. Hopefully we'll be able to use it in the morning."

"But of course you can't tell me where it was."

Liam chuckled. "Exactly, but I can tell you it involved water and maybe a stunt or two."

"Ooh, I'm intrigued"

"Maybe you should start watching the show then." Liam mused. For some reason he really wanted her to watch the show. At least a couple of episodes.

Abigail ignored the comment. "Do you do your own stunts?"

"I do what the studio will allow me to do. But some stunts, they outright refuse to even let me try."

"Well, speaking from a totally selfish perspective I'm glad they keep you on a tight leash."

"Oh, so you want me tied with a leash do you?" Liam chuckled. His Irish brogue oozed from every word.

"Oh my god no! That's not what I meant!" Even over the phone Liam knew just how to make Abigail blush. He was also good at making her picture him in naughty positions. She bit her lip slightly. "So something involving water, are you a good swimmer?"

Liam smiled knowing he had ruffled her in the best way possible which is why she had changed the subject. He would let her off the hook for now. "Yes, I swim very well. I was actually on my high school swim team for two years, until I got bored with it."

"So, not a team player?"

"Oh I was, but I was more into girls and soccer by the end of second year. What about you? Are you a swimmer?"

Abigail took a sip of her tea, "Very much so, always been a water baby. I'm a regular mermaid."

"Ah, so I wouldn't have to worry about you falling overboard and not being able to swim."

"Are we on a boat or cruise ship?"

Liam thought about that for a moment. "Not, sure yet, either I guess."

"Well, as long as I don't hit my head on the way down. I'll be fine."

"Good to know." Liam thought about taking Abigail on a cruise maybe around next Christmas to someplace warm and tropical. The thought took him off guard since he hadn't even seen her since their first encounter and here he was thinking about taking her on a trip. He absentmindedly pulled at his lower lip but stopped himself after a minute.

"Where did you go? I feel like you are further away than Toronto," Abigail asked.

"Sorry, I was just thinking about you in the water."

"I almost drowned once."

That got Liam's attention. "What? How?"

"It happened a long time ago. I was maybe seven. I was coming out of the water and a wave got me from behind, knocked me on my ass and took me back out with it."

"Oh my god! That must have been terrible."

Abigail shrugged. "Not really, Oddly enough I was really calm and I held my breath until the wave spit me rightside up. The scariest part was being so far from where my parents had been. I lost my bearings and it took me a while to walk all the way back to them."

"They didn't come looking for you?" Liam was confused by this."

Abigail sighed into the phone. "I learned at a very early age to rely on myself."

"Well, now you can rely on me too. I'll always have your back, waves be damned."

Abigail's voice caught in her throat for a moment. She actually believed he would. "Thank you." Nothing else needed to be said.

# CHAPTER TEN

A month and a half went by quickly. Abigail wasn't sure which made her happier, the knowledge that her kids were beginning to grasp Chaucer or that she would be seeing Liam in less than twenty-four hours. Endless hours of daily phone calls, intimate emails, and several facetimes could not make up for a flesh and blood person standing in front of her. Liam had teased her about not sharing his opinion of her writing until he saw her in person. She was dying to know his thoughts, but on the upside, it did give them a lot of time to just talk and get to know each other. But Abigail still wasn't brave enough to divulge the full truth to Liam. And she knew the longer she waited the worse it would be.

No homework would be assigned this weekend. It was the last period of the day and Abigail sat at her desk grading the pop-quiz she had just given while her students were working on a poem assignment. As she handed them back, she made one last announcement. "Don't forget auditions for the spring play are today after school. There will be more on Monday if you can't make it today but are interested in trying out. I know some of you are disappointed we aren't doing a musical. But with our musical director out on maternity leave, it just isn't possible. But *Merry Widows, Merry Brides* is a very funny play that I'm sure you'll enjoy being a part of."

The bell rang, and even though Abigail had more to say, it was Friday and as soon as the chime of that bell went off, her students' ears shut down as well as their brains. Their only thoughts were of the weekend out in the weather that was finally beginning to consistently stay warm and sunny. "Have a good weekend," she shouted as they filed out the door. Abigail couldn't get the smile off her face as she headed to the auditorium for the auditions. There was already a group of drama students gathering. Margot, who was acting as her assistant director, was there handing out slides.

"Thank you all for coming. Margot will call you in one at a time to audition. Cast list will be posted Tuesday morning. Good luck to you all." With that Abigail entered the auditorium and got herself set up to hear the same couple of monologues and scenes over and over for the next two hours. She looked at her phone one last time before they began.

\* \* \*

It was between takes and the shooting day was almost done. Only one last scene to shoot for the day and Liam would be heading to the airport to fly out to Connecticut. His head was in battle between trying to stay in the moment of the scenes and thinking about Abigail and what he should or shouldn't do. "Oh man, I'm in trouble." Liam turned to his co-star and friend Ted Randfell. He played the popular character Flint on the show. "Teddy, what am I going to do?"

"What's up man? Worried about your plans for the weekend? You can always come with me and Connie. We're heading to Montreal. Do a little dining, a little wining. You know, straight up R&R."

"That sounds lovely, but I'm going down to Connecticut."

Ted whistled. "Really, back to see that woman you were telling me about. Amy, no, Abi!"

"Yeah, god, I must be crazy to think about starting something."

"Woah! When you mean start something, are you talking a nice booty call whenever you have the time and an itch to scratch?"

"No man, I'm talking about something, something. I'm talking it's absolutely bonkers how immediately I was attracted to this lass and on such a deeper level than just the physical, and man is she gorgeous!"

"No offense, but I saw a picture of the two of you and she seems, let's just say she is not the average woman you've dated in the past."

"Why? Because she isn't some stick model?" Liam almost growled.

"Hey man! Don't get mad. I'm just stating the obvious."

Liam sighed. "Sorry, I didn't mean to bite your head off. I know, I know she isn't the usual type of woman I flash on the red carpet. But to be honest it's the type I've liked all along and didn't allow myself to be with after my career took off. I'm embarrassed to admit I listened to the wrong people, but now I don't care what people say or think. I care about what I want. I'm getting thoughts and feelings I haven't had since, since—"

"Since Miss Bianca Monroe."

"Right." Liam nodded.

"Yup, you're in trouble." Ted patted Liam's arm. "Look Liam, if you really are into this Abi woman then I say go for it. Take it one day at a time and just enjoy it. You deserve some happiness."

Liam smiled. "I do, don't I?"

"It's been long enough man. It's time. Oh wait, is she a fan of the show? She's not like some stalker in disguise or something?"

Liam chuckled. "That's the best part mate. She doesn't even watch the show. She's more of a reader, and a theatre goer than a sci-fi fantasy gal."

"Then I say, have a great weekend."

* * *

The auditions went well. There were some good choices in the group that came through. But Abigail and Margot promised each other not to have anyone set in mind until they saw all the auditions. They had one more day on Monday before they would make their decisions. "So Margot. Are you getting a taste for directing?"

Margot laughed. "I'm not sure about that, but I do like the casting part."

"I'm going to ask you one last time. Are you sure you don't want to audition yourself? I can direct by myself if you want to throw your hat in the ring."

Margot shook her head. "No, if we were doing a musical, I'd be all about it, but I was in the fall play. Being your assistant gives me something new to try."

"Alright, as long as you're sure. Then I'll see you Monday in class, and after school for the rest of the auditions. Have a great weekend, Margot."

"You too Miss Reese. Any big plans?" Margot asked with a sly smile on her face.

"Who knows?" Abigail gave her a wink. "See you Monday."

Abigail gave Margot a final wave and headed for the grocery store. She still needed to get things for her special Saturday dinner. She had gone back and forth in her mind what exactly she wanted to serve. At this point the only thing she was sure of is that she wanted to make some charlotte russe for dessert, and a nice garden salad.

Over the years, she had managed to have a very nice window box garden that stretched across the three windows of her living room. She had a small balcony on her fifth story apartment so she had access to them from both sides. She had been able to grow some lovely herbs as well as some cherry tomatoes, some carrots, and some kale. With the help of a small hothouse that the landlord had looked the other way on, her fresh vegetables were at her disposal almost year round now. She thanked her father for teaching her how to have a green thumb. It paid off well in the winter months. She picked up some freshly made french bread. Maybe she would go Italian and make some homemade garlic bread. But they did go to an Italian restaurant on their first date.

She shook her head. She still couldn't believe what she just had been thinking about, the '*first date*'. She cleared her head and wandered through the meat and seafood sections to see if anything jumped out at her. Maybe a beef wellington? Or shrimp and grits? Lobster tails and scallops? Or maybe some juicy crab legs with drawn butter? Abigail imagined watching Liam suck the meat from deep inside the leg of a crab. Maybe see a single drip of butter that he licked up with his tongue. Yes, the thought took her breath away. Crabs legs it would be, and the garlic bread and salad would go perfectly with them. She picked up several pounds of snow crab legs and then headed home.

Abigail could feel her phone vibrating in her pocket as she unlocked her front door. She quickly put her bags on the kitchen island and pulled her phone out of her pocket. "Hello?" she practically shouted.

"Hello lovely."

Abigail smiled when she heard Liam's voice. "I was just thinking about you."

"Oh really? What were you thinking?" Liam asked. He had been thinking his own thoughts about Abi, some of them sweet and some very very naughty.

"I'm not sure if I should tell you." Abi laughed.

"Well. if you don't want to share, I'll just leave it to my imagination."

Abigail bit her lip, wondering what wonderful things his imagination could lead to. She snapped herself out of it. "So, have you left for the airport yet?"

"Actually that's what I'm calling about. There has been a change in plans."

Abigail tried not to sound disappointed. She thought he might be canceling. It would make sense if he was changing his mind. The trip was a little much for only the weekend which didn't even come to two full days together with all the travel time. "Okay, did your work schedule change or something?

"As a matter of fact it did."

"That's okay, I understand."

Liam couldn't help but smile. He could tell she thought he was backing out. He wouldn't torture her any longer, well, not about this anyway. "I'm glad you feel that way because I was able to catch an earlier flight and I'm already at the hotel. Care to go for dinner? I'm starving."

"Oh!" Abigail laughed. "That's not what I was expecting you to hear. But yes, I would love to go to dinner with you. "

"I can pick you up in say half an hour?"

"That sounds perfect."

"Alright, I just need your address and I'll see you in thirty minutes."

Abigail gave him her address and hung up. She couldn't stop smiling as she put the rest of the groceries away and tidied up her apartment a little. She wasn't expecting him to see it until tomorrow but she had already started the cleaning process so there wasn't much left to do. Once that was done, she realized she only had ten minutes left to get ready.

# CHAPTER ELEVEN

◆———————◆

Abigail jumped in the shower for a quick wash down. Five minutes later she was out of the shower and fully lotioned. She could thank years of being a summer camp counselor for her ability to take quick showers. Standing in front of her closet, she debated on what to wear. She decided to go with something casual, but pretty. It was a little chilly for a sundress and she didn't know where he wanted to take her, so she decided on a flowy green skirt that went down to her knees. It kind of resembled a peasant skirt but a little more classy because of the material used and the lace trim on the bottom. For the top she chose a simple black v-neck. It showed off her cleavage quite well.

She always got a look or two when she wore it. It was also great because it showed off her necklace, another wonderful gift from Tess, it was a beautiful Celtic knot design in rose gold. She was putting on her lipstick when the door buzzer went off. She went into the living room and hit the intercom button. "Hello?"

"It's me, can I come up?"

Abigail buzzed him in. A few minutes later, there was a knock at her door. Abigail opened it to see a smiling Liam with a small bouquet of flowers. "Hello my lovely." He handed the flowers to Abigail.

She took a big whiff and smiled. "You're going to spoil me if you keep giving me flowers."

He entered, shutting the door behind him. "Beautiful ladies deserve beautiful flowers."

Abigail gave him a quick kiss on the lips. "Thank you so much. I'll just go put these in water. Come in, make yourself comfortable." Abigail went to the kitchen. She pulled down a vase from the top of the fridge and some scissors from a drawer. She ran the stems under the water and cut them on a diagonal like her father had taught her. She was putting them in the vase when Liam came up behind her and wrapped his arms around her waist. He began kissing her neck. She sucked in her breath at the sensation. She almost dropped the vase.

"Hi," he whispered between kisses. "I didn't realize how much I missed you until you opened the door." He gripped her hips and gently bit her shoulder before going back to kissing it. He snaked his hand over her shoulder and down her v-neck. He caressed her breast over her bra. His height really was an advantage as he licked her ear.

Abigail moaned, "I missed you too. "

Liam turned her around and took her face in his hands. He dropped little kisses over her eyes and her forehead, and down her cheeks. She was getting dizzy with all the sensations that were zipping through her body. "I, I thought you were starving."

Liam looked into her chocolate brown eyes, licked his lips and winked. "I am." He planted a kiss on her lips demanding entrance. She moaned and opened her mouth to him, letting their tongues entwine. Liam pressed his entire body against Abigail so she could feel just how happy he was to see her.

Abigail grabbed his ass, drawing him even closer. He groaned as he grinded up against her. He moved her v-neck over a little, exposing her bra. He moved that aside, giving her exposed breast tiny butterfly kisses. Abigail arched her back wanting more. "Couch," she whispered as she bit his ear. Liam took her hand and led her to the couch. He sat her down and began kissing her. She drew him down on top of her. He stopped for a moment sitting up so he could take her shirt off. He kissed her neck as he unhooked her bra. His hands immediately went to her small yet supple breast. For a plus size woman she had smaller breasts than most would assume, but they were perfect for him. He kneaded them in his hand as he kissed and licked at her neck.

Abigail tried to get his shirt off. Finally he took it off for her, showing off his six pack. She gently ran her fingernails over it before she began kissing it. Liam pulled her face up to his and began kissing her again, biting her lower lip before drawing her tongue into his mouth so he could suck on it, gently moving her further down on the couch. He started kissing down her body, stopping at her breasts. Liam took his time kissing and licking at each one before taking one in his mouth and gently sucking on it and then the other, loving the sounds coming from Abigail as his tongue swirled around each nipple. He could tell she was going to be loud when he finally made her come. The thought only made him harder. He bit her nipple making her cry out, arching her back even more.

Abigail was getting so wet, but she wasn't sure if she wanted to sleep with him just yet. But he felt so good on top of her and she could feel that he was rock hard. She wanted him inside her so badly. But this was still so new. Was it too soon?

Liam could tell something was off. "Abi, are you alright? Do you want me to stop?"

Abigail took a moment to catch her breath. "No, I mean yes, I mean, you feel so good, but I don't know."

Liam had been raised with a very respectful father, a loving mother and two sisters. He knew that the only yes was a yes. Maybe, or I don't know, meant no. He immediately stopped and sat up. "Talk to me, what's going on?" He wrapped a blanket that was on the couch over her shoulders so she could cover up. He ran his hand through his hair, trying to slow his breath and calm himself.

"Can I ask you something and I need you to be completely honest with me?"

"Of course."

"Am I just a booty call for you? Am I your chance at a fat girl conquest?"

Liam was stunned by her words. Where on earth were they coming from? They had talked every day since he had sent her the photographs. They had shared a lot. "Abi, I would never treat you like that. Nor do I even think of you like that."

"How do you think of me?"

Liam took her hand and kissed it. "I think of you as a lovely woman who I am sharing what I hope will be a very long and very loving relationship with. I think of you as the person I need and deserve in my life."

Abigail tried not to cry at his words. He made her feel so beautiful and so desirable. It had been a very long time since anyone had made her feel like that. She grabbed his face and kissed him. "You are so incredibly special to me." She kissed him again drawing him down on top of her, wrapping her legs around his waist.

They kissed for a while until Liam pulled back. "Abi, not that I don't love making out with you, but if we don't stop soon, I'm going to want to taste you, and more."

Abigail smiled and gave him one last kiss. "Okay, then we should stop. I'm not quite ready for more yet. I want more, but not yet. Is that okay?"

Liam pulled her up, so they were both in a sitting position. "That's perfectly fine, my lovely." He bent down to pick up his shirt and put it back on. "But we still have a problem."

Abigail just watched him cover up his beautiful body. "And that is?"

"I'm still starving."

Abigail laughed. "How about we order some food? How do you feel about Thai food?"

"Sounds perfect."

They ordered food and decided to eat in the living room while watching some shows on DTV. When dinner was done, Abigail made them ice cream sundaes. Abigail scooped a dollop of ice cream and made sure there was some whipped cream and caramel on it. She held it up to Liam. "Taste?" She had caramel ice cream. He had chocolate.

Liam opened his mouth for her. She gently put the spoonful of ice cream goodness in his mouth. He closed his eyes as he closed his mouth around the spoon. She pulled it out slowly. "Mmm, that tastes good."

"Want some more?"

"I'll take another spoonful." Liam smiled.

Abigail put a spoonful in her mouth and then kissed Liam, sharing the ice cream with him. He deepened the kiss, grabbing her shoulder, almost massaging it. He groaned as he pulled away. "You are killing me, woman."

"Sorry, I don't mean to. I just like kissing you." She nuzzled his nose with hers.

"I know the feeling." He kissed her some more. They eventually broke apart. "I should get going. It's late."

"You could stay."

Liam smiled. "I would love to, but I don't know if I can trust myself. You are quite irresistible, you know."

"How about we go to the farmers market tomorrow? Or maybe the movies before I cook you dinner?"

"Either one is fine with me. Or we can do both if we start early enough." Liam got up and tucked his shirt inside his pants. "I can pick you up at ten?"

"Ten, I like ten. That works for me." She wrapped her hands around his waist and kissed him. Soft kisses. He kissed her back just as softly.

"I'm going to leave now. Because I'm a minute away from taking you to your bedroom," Liam stated between kisses.

Abigail sighed as he pulled away. It wasn't fair of her to tease him and she knew it. "Alright, go get some rest, and I'll see you at ten sharp." She gave him one last kiss and walked him to the door.

# CHAPTER TWELVE

———◆———

The next morning Liam was true to his word, ten am sharp there was a buzz at Abigail's door. She let him into the building. "Door is unlocked, just come on in," she said into the buzzer. Liam entered her apartment to find her at the hall mirror pulling her hair up into a ponytail.

"I really do love your braids." He twirled a couple between his hands as he gave her a kiss. "Good morning, my lovely. How did you sleep?"

"Oh, nice sunglasses. I slept very well, how about you?"

"Sweet, sweet dreams." Liam gave her a wink. He clapped his hands together. "Come, let's start our day, shall we?" He pulled a baseball cap out of his back pocket.

Abigail just looked at him and he just shrugged. She smiled. "I get it." She grabbed her purse and his hand. "Come on."

They stopped for coffee at a little shop around the corner of her apartment before walking the five blocks to the market in the park. Abigail was giddy as it was the first market of the season now that spring had officially sprung. They picked up some fresh flowers and some pretzels. They grabbed some apricots and raw honey as well as some heavy cream from a dairy farmer and some of his coffee milk. Abigail was no stranger to this market, so she knew to bring some cloth bags with her to carry whatever goodies she gathered. She often brought ice packs with her as well, today those packs were coming in handy.

They stopped at a booth that had some wonderful homemade essential oils. Abigail picked up some honeysuckle and Liam got himself some patchouli. "I should have known that you would like essential oils." Liam smiled. The more he was learning about Abigail the more he liked her. As Abigail was paying, he saw a young woman, a teenager really, staring at them out of the corner of his eye. He grabbed Abigail's hand and started moving along to some other booths. He could see the girl was following them. He pulled Abigail a little closer. She stopped at another booth to look at some used books. That is when the person following them approached Liam.

"Excuse me, are you Liam Caffney?"

Abigail looked up from the books she was looking at. Liam patted her hand signaling her that everything was fine. He put on his best smile. "Yes, I am."

The girl smiled and started gushing immediately. "Oh my god I thought it was you! What are you doing here?! I love you on the show! I really hope Lochlan and Beatrice end up together. Isla isn't good enough for you. I mean Lochlan. Oh my god! I can't believe I'm standing in front of you right now! Can you give me any hints for next season?"

"Woah there, now why don't we start with your name?"

"Oh yes! Sorry," she giggled. "My name is Nina, I'm Nina. I'm a huge fan! Probably one of your biggest. I even run a fan site about the show. It's called 'Lochlan of EverMorph'. Have you seen it? You probably haven't, but that's okay. Can I get a picture with you? I can't wait to post this." Nina spoke a mile a minute.

More people started to notice what was happening. This Nina girl seemed to be getting louder and louder the more she talked. And she seemed to have quite a lot to say. She had to be around fifteen, or sixteen and she had the teen squeal down pat.

Abigail saw the other people taking note and it made her a bit nervous. There was no security here. They were in an open park. What if more people mobbed him? This Nina girl seemed to be shrieking. At least that's what it sounded like to her. This was a perfect example of why she didn't want to be associated with fans. It was because of shrieking girls like this, or the ones who didn't know the difference between the character and the actor. People like that were thought of as the rule, not the exception. "Liam?"

Liam turned slightly and saw the look on Abigail's face. She wasn't used to this yet. He pulled her close to him, taking her hand. "Nina, this is my girl Abi. I'm sure she would be happy to take the picture you requested. Right, Abi?" He squeezed her hand.

Abigail took a deep breath and smiled. "Yes, of course. I take it you are a fan of *EverMorphs*?" She tried to act like she was having trouble remembering the name of the show.

Nina looked at her like she had three heads, but she handed Abigail her phone anyway to take the picture. She moved away from Liam as Nina moved closer so that she could take the picture.

"Okay, smile." Abigail snapped a picture.

"Take another one, will you Abi please?" Liam put both of his arms around Nina in a side hug. She looked like she was in heaven.

Abigail could tell this picture would be blown up, framed, and hung relatively close to Nina's bed. Abigail took two more photos and then handed Nina her phone back. "It was very nice to meet you, Nina. I hope you like the pictures I took."

Nina looked at the photos on her phone and grinned ear to ear. "They are perfect, thank you so much."

"Anytime." Abigail nodded and then turned back to the owner of the booth to pay for the books she had set aside. She wanted to give Liam a moment to say goodbye to Nina in private.

Liam was signing the hat Nina had on when she looked over at Abigail. "Wait, you said she was your girl? The woman who took the picture for me, is she your new girlfriend?"

Liam looked over at Abigail and winked. He turned back to Nina with a big smile on his face. "Well yes, yes she is. And as my biggest fan you are officially the first person to know. But can you keep it a secret? Just for a little while."

Nina looked Abigail up and down several times. She seemed to approve. "Of course I can."

"Oh, thank you darlin'. Now we've got to be going, but it was very nice meeting you, Nina." Liam took Abigail's hand as she moved toward them, putting the books in one of her bags.

"Bye!" Nina waved as they walked away. She immediately got on her phone. Liam could hear her as she walked away "OMG Stacy! You'll never guess who I just met!"

Liam put his arm around Abigail as they continued walking away.

Abigail turned to Liam "So, I'm your girl, am I? You know she took pictures of us walking away."

"Ay, I'm aware. I'm also sure she won't keep seeing us together a secret." He stopped her for a moment taking both of her hands in his. "I'm sorry. I know we haven't really talked about what we are. If there even is an 'us' in that way. But that's how I think of you. I've felt like that since I stepped off the plane. You're my girl and it's time people knew it."

Abigail kissed him and stroked his cheek. "I like being 'your girl'." She kissed him again.

Liam l felt like his heart was opening up. Like it was softening again. He kissed her, deepening it and holding her close. He didn't care who saw it. Abigail began to moan softly as she felt like she was melting into him. He finally had to pull away. "We should head back to your apartment, but take the long way back."

"You don't want to see the rest of the market?"

Liam shook his head. "I can guess that Nina called all of her friends and they will soon descend upon this lovely market. I'd rather not be here for that, and I can guarantee neither do you."

Abigail nodded in agreement. She followed Liam's lead as he made an eight block loop back to her apartment. Abigail put her purchases away before heading out to the movies. Liam drove as Abigail gave him directions as he drove. He kept his hand in hers the entire ride.

Abigail had picked a theatre that showed old movies. It was a sure way she wouldn't run into any of her students at the theater. "How old school do you want to go?" Abigail asked as Liam parked the car.

"What do you mean?"

"Well we can go back to the fifties and watch *Singin' in the Rain*. But that's a musical, so if you don't like them we should skip it. We can go back to the seventies and watch *Jaws*. Or we could go way way back and see *The Death Kiss*. A mystery from the thirties."

"Hmm, they all sound interesting. Although I haven't seen many musicals in my lifetime. So I'm not sure how much I'll like it. What do you want to see?"

"It's your weekend. You choose." Abigail smiled.

"Okay, then let's go with *Jaws*."

Abigail took his hand and led him into the theater. "*Jaws* it is."

# CHAPTER THIRTEEN

—◆————————◆—

"Come on, tell me you wouldn't scream like that if a great white was trying to eat you." Liam chuckled.

"I'm sorry, I love the movie, but I don't think the scream was realistic. I never thought it was," Abigail stated as she opened her apartment door. "Make yourself at home. I need to start dinner. Can I get you something to drink?"

"Anything you have is fine." Liam made himself comfortable on the couch.

"Do you prefer alcoholic or non-alcoholic?" Abigail called from the kitchen.

"Let's go with non-alcoholic drinks for now. I like to drink with dinner."

"Good point," Abigail said as she came into the living room with a glass of ice tea. She even had a lemon wedge on the edge of the glass.

Liam took the glass and put it down on the coffee table. He pulled Abigail down on the couch and began kissing her. He slid his hands under her shirt. He caressed her back for a while before trying to undo her bra. He was having trouble and it made Abigail laugh. "I'm taking this as a sign we should stop."

Liam nuzzled her neck giving it little kisses and gentle bites as he went. It made Abigail sigh. Her breathing was becoming raspy. "Are you sure you want me to stop?" He put her hand on his cock that was beginning to get hard. She gave it a gentle squeeze and began rubbing it through his jeans. He groaned, squeezing her shoulder. His lips met hers. Each opening their mouth to the other. Tongues entangled, both breathing heavier.

A buzzer went off in the kitchen. Abigail sighed as she slowly pulled away. "The water is ready for the crab."

"No, stay with me." Liam kissed her again.

Abigail laughed. "There will be plenty of time for this later."

Liam raised an eyebrow. "Is that a promise?"

Abigail winked as she headed to the kitchen. "We'll see."

Abigail took a long sip of ice tea once she had put the crab legs in. Liam was making her very hot, and it was becoming hard to resist him. And if she was honest with herself, she really didn't want to. After she had made the garlic bread, she put it in foil and set it aside. It wasn't time to go into the oven yet.

She started on the salad. "Liam, can you grab some tomatoes from the balcony for me?" She waited for an answer but didn't get one. "Liam?" Abigail walked into the living room. Liam was asleep curled under the blanket she kept on the couch; Beatrice was curled up on his hip. She watched him for a minute and smiled. A runaway curl had fallen on his face. She gently tucked it behind his ear and kissed his forehead. "What am I going to do with you? You are capturing my heart minute by minute," she whispered. She kissed his forehead and headed to the balcony to grab some tomatoes.

Liam opened his eyes as she walked away. "I know the feeling," he whispered. He closed his eyes again, falling back to sleep.

When dinner was ready, Abigail went into the living room to wake Liam up. But he was already up reading *The Canterbury Tales,* as he gave some love to Lochlan.

"That's one of my favorites. But I think you know that already." Abigail smiled.

"Your help has been invaluable. It would have stayed a jumbled mess without you. Is your class still on *The Pardoner's Tale?*"

"We finished that tale. We're on *The Wife of Bath.* My seniors are having a really hard time with it. I'm trying to make it easier for them but it's a challenge. Hey, dinner is ready."

Liam put the book down and followed her into the dining room. "I'm starving. What did you—" He stopped when he saw the table setting. Abigail had put the flowers from the market in a vase on the table. She had cut them nice and low so that they could see each other. She had also set out some candles and dimmed the lights. Fancy wine glasses were filled with what he could only imagine was one of their favorite wines. She had obviously put out the good china as well, salad bowls included. Liam whistled. "Wow, this looks amazing! Did you do all of this while I was sleeping?"

Abigail nodded as she set the still warm garlic bread on the table. "I even pre-cracked the crab."

"Careful Abi, you're spoiling me. I might get used to it."

Abigail kissed his cheek before sitting down. "Good! Now let's dig in."

Dinner was going well. The crab had cooked perfectly.

"So tell me, why were you reading *The Pardoner's Tale*? It isn't your average light reading."

Liam put his fork down. "Okay, so what I am about to say you cannot tell anyone. I can trust you right?"

"Of course."

"I'm shooting a new television series and it's based on *The Canterbury Tales*. I'll be playing the Pardoner in this new updated sci-fi version."

"You're leaving your current show?" Abigail practically shouted.

Liam looked at her for a moment. It wasn't the response he

was expecting. "No, not at all. This is just a small little project between seasons. I have no intention of leaving EverMorphs anytime soon."

"Oh, okay." Abigail tried to play it off cool. She didn't think it was working.

"But there is more."

"Am I going to like it?"

Liam shrugged. "I hope so."

"Don't keep me in suspense. Tell me."

Liam took a sip of wine to draw out the suspense.

"Don't make me pout Liam. You wouldn't like me when I pout." Abigail stuck her lower lip out.

Liam laughed. "You look hot even when you pout. Especially that bottom lip of yours, it's just begging to be bit."

"Liam, tell me."

"Okay, sorry. What I wanted to tell you was that it is filming for two months about an hour north of here."

"Wait, what?" Abigail needed him to say it again. Just to be sure she heard him correctly.

"I will be only one hour away from you for two months. I have two months of filming left in Toronto and then two weeks off and then filming. Just sixty short minutes away." He smiled.

"So I get you almost all summer?" Abigail was trying to contain her excitement.

Liam nodded. "But I do have some contest things I have to participate in somewhere in there. The winner hasn't been picked yet so I don't know where I'll be flying. So, I'll be gone for a couple of days for that. The show is sponsoring it. They are hoping it will help the arts in public schools."

Abigail nodded. "They need it. They are always the first programs cut, but the ones most needed."

"I was hoping maybe I could just stay here with you on my days off?"

Abigail nodded. "I would really really love that."

They talked about anything and everything while they finished their dinner.

Finally Abigail couldn't take it anymore, and she had to ask. "So you promised to tell me what you thought about what I sent you to read."

Liam looked at her as he took a sip of this wine. He could see the apprehension in her face, she didn't share her writing very often. She was genuinely worried he wouldn't like it. She had no idea how truly talented she was. He needed to change that. Liam reached out for her hand and kissed it. "If I had only one day to capture the essence of your bloom, to memorize the soft ebb and flow of each delicate petal. To ingrain the luscious scent that emanates from your core into my senses for all time, it wouldn't be enough. For you are timeless, and sadly I am out of time."

Abigail was shocked and wasn't sure how to respond. He was quoting from the poem she had sent him. She was speechless, all she could do was blush, an act he could not possibly see.

Liam gave her hand a squeeze. "They were all lovely, so full of life, passion, and dare I say pain. You really have a wonderful way of creating a world that anyone would long to be a part of, even in the tragic moments. I shed several tears when Anastasia lost her sweet babe."

A smile swept across Abigail's face as she let out the breath she had been holding. "I'm so glad you liked them."

Liam shook his head. "I didn't like them, I loved them. In fact, I passed one of your stories to Leenie, and she agreed with me. She asked if she could give it to an agent friend of hers, and I said yes."

"Why? What? Why did you do that? That was only for you!" Abigail drained her wine glass and poured herself some more.

"Please don't be mad, they were just so wonderful." Liam was hesitant to tell her the rest, but he had to. "But the good news is that her agent friend really liked it. She wants to meet you."

Abigail wasn't sure if she should be upset or elated. Liam had believed enough in her and her writing enough to pass it along to someone in the industry that could actually make it go somewhere. She had no words so she just leaned over and kissed him. "Thank you," she whispered as she looked into his eyes.

"I'll take it, you're not mad then?" Liam kissed her back.

Abigail shook her head. "I am so far from mad."

"Then you should be hearing from Deana Cartwhile probably in the next week. I'll let Leenie know it's okay to give her your phone number."

Abigail nodded. "Please thank Leenie for me. But for now, how about dessert in the living room?" Abigail asked as she started to clear the table.

"That sounds wonderful but let me clean up love. You made such a lovely dinner, it's the least I can do."

Abigail couldn't believe what he just said. He had called her love. Her heart skipped a beat. "Thank you. I'll just get dessert started then."

Liam cleared the dishes, rinsed, and put them in the dishwasher. He wiped down the table and moved the candles into the living room. In the meantime Abigail got out two dessert cups and filled it with charlotte russe. It was a dessert her mother had taught her how to make. It was either chocolate or vanilla cakes doused in either homemade vanilla whipped cream or homemade chocolate whipped cream. It was always best to do the opposite for the cake and whipped cream. Abigail had decided on vanilla cake and chocolate whipped cream. She dished it out and then made some amaretto coffees to go with them. She set up everything on a tray and brought it into the living room. Abigail smiled when she saw what he had done, she loved the way he had set up the room.

Liam had made a little pillow nest for them using the lip of the couch as a place to lean pillows against. He'd pulled pillows from the couch as well as from her bedroom. He had also set some blankets around and had turned the tv to a music station playing contemporary classics. Abigail set the dessert tray on the coffee table.

"This nest is amazing, and I love the candles. Do you mind if I change before we eat? I want to be nice and cozy."

"Not at all love. Do whatever makes you comfortable."

Abigail went into her bedroom, closing the door behind her. She put on a pair of sleep shorts and a sleep tank top. It was yellow with some light orange flowers on it, and although it wasn't silk, it was a shiny fabric that was cool and silky to the touch. She put her hair up in a loose ponytail with a braid or two flowing freely and walked back out into the living room.

Liam was already sitting in the nest sipping his coffee. He whistled as she walked out. "Love, you look amazing."

She sat down next to him. "It's just some jammies. "

"I like your jammies then." He put the blanket he had over his legs over Abigail's as well. "May I?" He pointed to the dessert. He didn't want to start without her.

"Please." She handed him one of the cups and she took the other.

He took a bite. "Mmm, this is so good! I've never tasted something like this before."

"It's a family recipe. My mom taught me how to make it when I was around ten. It's one of my favorites. But I only make it for special occasions."

Liam cocked his head to the side. "So, I'm a special occasion?"

"Maybe." Abigail smiled.

They ate in silence for a few minutes enjoying the music. Liam broke the silence. "Can I ask you something?"

"Anything."

"I know you aren't a fan of *The EverMorphs*. But are you a fan of anything?"

Abigail shook her head. "No, not anymore."

"What do you mean, not anymore?"

Abigail sighed. "I don't like being thought of as a fan. So I try not to like anything too much to be classified as one, or called one, or thought of as one, or treated like one." She was visibly upset.

"Hey, it's okay. We don't have to talk about it." He scooped her up in his arms. He just stayed like that until he could feel her body start to calm and relax itself. "I feel like there is a story here. But you don't have to tell me until you are ready. Just know that I am here."

Abigail looked into Liam's eyes. She wanted to tell him what had happened to her all those years ago. What had made her start to hide what she was a fan of and confess just how much she loved his show and his talent. But she didn't dare, instead she kissed him.

She kissed him with all the feelings she longed to tell him but was afraid to say. She wrapped her hands around his head playing with his curls as they kissed. Abigail wanted more so she deepened the kiss. She leaned back, taking Liam with her. She loved to feel his weight on top of her. Abigail squeezed his ass as she kissed his neck and ear and then back to his mouth. She ran her hands down his back, pulling his shirt out of his jeans.

Liam leaned them both up. He took his shirt off and then pulled her tank top off. He cupped her breasts and caressed them as he looked into her eyes. Liam relished rubbing his thumbs over her nipples making them hard. Abigail sucked in her breath as a sensual current shot through her. She ran his hands over his chest, enjoying the feel of each muscle.

Liam kissed down her neck and down her chest, her belly and then back up again. He stopped at her breasts, giving them ample attention. His tongue was like electricity making a fiery current run through her entire body.

Abigail reached down to unzip his pants. Reaching in, she was shocked at how long he was. He was getting hard under her touch. She began stroking him, making him moan. "Take them off, please," Abigail whispered.

Liam looked at her for a moment. "Are you sure, Abi?"

Abigail kissed him, biting his lower lip. "Yes."

There was a twinkle in Liam's eye. "I will if you will."

"Take them off for me?" Abigail purred.

Liam stood up and slowly took his jeans off. Never taking his eyes off of Abigail. It was no surprise to her that he was going commando. He moved the coffee table out more towards the center of the room. He wanted space to move with Abigail. Liam kneeled down, he stroked her body from the neck down. When he reached her waist, he gathered her shorts in his hands and slowly began to pull them down.

She lifted her hips allowing him to pull them down below her ass. He finished pulling them down her thighs and calves and then they were off. Liam took a moment and stared at her body. He wanted to memorize every curve, every roll, every dimple. He loved them all. "You are truly beautiful," Liam murmured as he kissed and licked his way up her body. He found her lips and began kissing her again. He loved the way her tongue tasted and felt. He skipped his way down her body. Using his knee, he spread her legs apart. He ran his hand up her inner thigh. Liam ran his hand along her slit. It was nice and slick.

Abigail sucked in her breath at his touch. It had been a while since she had been intimate with someone and Liam knew how to make her body tingle like no other. She wanted him, and now that he felt just how wet she was, he knew it too.

Liam dipped a finger between her nether lips, looking for her pearl. It was already hot and vibrating. Abigail bucked and moaned as he began to stroke it. She raised her hips, wanting him to go deeper. "Patience, my sweet Abi," Liam huskily whispered.

Abigail gripped the blankets as Liam played. Breathing heavily, she loved and hated the teasing. Liam moved his hand to his mouth, licking his fingers. He smiled, giving

Abigail a wink. "Mmm, delicious. Better than I dreamed." He repositioned himself kissing her belly. He kissed every inch of her belly before moving his head between her legs. He parted her lips giving her a slow, long lick.

"Liam, oh Liam," Abigail moaned. She reached for his head. She took a lock and started twirling it as she writhed beneath him.

Liam stroked her thighs as his tongue explored her. He relished in tasting her honey and eliciting the moans and sighs that he knew were bringing her closer to the edge. He stopped just short of her release of pleasure. She had a moment to catch her breath before his nimble fingers found what they were looking for.

Abigail arched her back and opened her hips wider to him, closing her eyes as she did.

"No love, don't close your eyes. Look at me. I want to see you. Really see you." He kissed her as let his fingers work their magic then went back to gazing in her eyes

Abigail opened her eyes and gazed at Liam. No one had ever asked her to do that. Abigail's breath became raspy. Her entire body was humming. It was almost like she was floating. She started to close eyes out of habit.

Liam saw her eyes beginning to shut and he stopped moving his fingers, leaving them in her warm folds with no movement. Abigail's eyes immediately snapped open. He looked at her for a moment. "Stay with me, love. Don't close your eyes." It wasn't a command, but it wasn't a request either. All Abigail could do was nod. "Good girl." Liam winked and started moving his fingers again.

Abigail was close to release. She reached for Liam's free hand, never breaking eye contact with him. "Liam, I'm— oh god!" She clasped his hand, interlocking their fingers. She squeezed hard as her orgasm took over, cascading throughout her body. She looked into his eyes the whole time, making the orgasm that much sweeter and longer. It had never been like this for her before.

As her orgasm began to subside Liam swiftly slipped his rock hard cock inside her, letting out a low groan as he did. He loved the way her wet pussy walls enveloped his cock. Abigail cried out in pleasure. He filled her perfectly, like they were always meant to combine and become one. Liam started thrusting within her, rolling his hips to hit every angle. He clasped Abigail's hands, putting them over her head and pinning them there. Leaning down he took a nipple in his mouth, making it his own. All Abigail could do was moan and submit, her hips thrusting up to meet him.

Liam kept adjusting his speed from slow deep thrusts to fast and furious and back down again. He knew just how to prolong their first time. Sweating and letting off moans and groans that were primitive and guttural, he finally spilled his seed within her only moments after she had screamed his name at her own powerful release. He collapsed on top of her, both of them out of breath. She covered his face in sweet kisses.

"Will you stay the night?" she asked. She wanted to wake up with him.

Liam grabbed a blanket and wrapped the two of them in it. "As long as you don't care if I sleep in the nude."

Abigail kissed him. "Not at all." She started to snuggle down.

"Would you be more comfortable if we moved the bedroom? Get into bed?"

Abigail shook her head and smiled. "Not just yet. I'm good right here."

"Your wish is my command." They snuggled down together. It wasn't long before they fell asleep.

The next morning there was a very loud knock on the door. It startled Abigail because she hadn't buzzed anyone up. She and Liam never made it to the bedroom. They had slept in their nest. Sometime in the middle of the night Lochlan and Beartice had joined them. They were currently curled up behind Liam's back. Abigail slipped her pajamas back on and quietly walked to the front door. "Who is it?"

"It's me! Open up, I brought breakfast," Tess barked through the door.

Abigail looked back at a sleeping Liam. He had begun to stir at the commotion. "Hang on just a minute!"

Abigail went and kissed Liam to wake him up. He pulled her down as he kept kissing her. She finally pulled away. "My friend Tess is here. She has breakfast. I'm sure it's because she wants to check you out."

Liam smiled. "This is best friend Tess, yes? Well then, I better put some clothes on." Liam grabbed his clothes and headed to the bathroom. Abigail went to open the door as she heard the shower turn on.

"That took you long enough," Tess started as she moved her head around looking for a glimpse of Liam.

"Good morning to you too. And he's in the shower so stop straining your neck."

"Oh, okay." Tess started emptying her bags. "So. I'm not interrupting anything then." Tess smiled.

"What exactly are you doing here?"

"Well, I figured the only way I would get to meet your hunky man in person was if I just popped on over. I thought breakfast would soften the blow." Tess laughed.

"You just couldn't wait a couple of more visits could you?"

"Um no, he lives too far away for that."

"Lives too far away for what?" Liam asked as he walked into the kitchen. He was rubbing his hair with a towel to get out the excess water. He draped the towel over the chair and put his arms out to hug Tess. "Tess, I'm so glad you are here. I've heard so much about you."

Tess hugged him back. "Back at you. Let me just say I'm a big fan of your work. And I brought breakfast, I hope you're hungry."

Liam gave her a great big smile. "I'm starving. Let me help you unpack."

Tess raised an eyebrow and looked at Abigail. "He helps in the kitchen?"

Abigail nodded. "He's good like that."

"What else is he good at?" Tess smirked as she looked Liam up and down.

Abigail slapped her arm. "I will throw you out if you don't behave."

"Now, now Abi, that's no way to treat your best friend. Besides, how else am I going to learn all of your secrets?" Liam winked at Tess.

"Sorry Liam, my lips are sealed. Breakfast is all you will get out of me."

Liam gave her a wink. "We'll see about that."

Tess was true to her word and didn't spill any juicy secrets even though Liam tried a couple of times as they ate. He really liked Tess. He could see why she was Abigail's best friend.

Tess put her dishes in the sink. "Okay kids, I won't take up anymore of your time. I know this is a short visit." She went to give Liam a hug good-bye.

"You don't have to leave because of me, Tess. I'll be around for a long time if Abi can stand me." He winked at Abigail.

Tess laughed. "Oh I know you'll be around a good long while. That's why I don't mind leaving now. I see a bright future for you kids." She gave Abigail a hug. "I'll call you later. Ta-ta for now!" Tess headed out the door.  A moment later she popped her head back in. "Oh, and if you two love birds go out today, may I suggest going out the back? There are some paparazzi waiting in the front."

Abigail was shocked. "What? How?"

Tess tried to downplay it. "Don't worry it's only like two guys." She blew Abigail a kiss as she closed and door behind her

Abigail got to work on cleaning off the table. Liam wrapped his arms around her. "I like Tess." He kissed her neck.

Abigail hugged his arms around her. "She likes you too. But not as much as I do."

The weekend passed by far too quickly for both Abigail and Liam. Abigail kissed him goodbye one last time before he headed to the airport with a promise from him that he would call when he landed. She missed him as soon as he shut the door behind him.

Ted picked Liam up from the airport. He threw his bag in the trunk before getting in. "Thanks for picking me up, mate."

"Not a problem. We got back in earlier this morning. Connie gave me strict instructions to bring you home for dinner. She wants to hear all about this mystery woman who has you racking up frequent flier miles."

Liam chuckled. "It was one weekend man!"

"So you won't be going back?"

A big smile spread across Liam's face. "Oh no, I'll be going back."

"Sounds like you have a lot to tell us."

Liam looked out the window. "Aye."

"Well, I'm happy for you man. Can't wait to hear all about it."

# CHAPTER FOURTEEN

*And That's All I Have To Say About That!*

*All Things EverMorph All the Time*

*S*eason Four - Episode Highlights: A new story arc is brewing centered around the disappearance of Flint, but the season is almost over? Will it spill into next season? Isla learns about the affair!! (well kinda sorta affair) Lowlights: It's becoming more and more obvious that Queen Ryla is an inconsistent character in the EverMorph world.

My humblest apologies to you my loyal Everrites and Morphlings for this late chit chat. But I am here now so let us chit and chat shall we? Up first.........FLINT!!!! Where is our dearest Flint and who has him? All I could glimpse from the last episode is that someone or something is holding him captive. And whatever it is has a dark *foreboding energy. Come on all my Flint Fairies, any guesses? Put them in the comments. I have a theory or two of my own, but I'm keeping them to myself for the time being. But I will tell you it's a doozy and very out of the box! However the REAL question has become: is Lochlan going to journey on to help save the human race from the Morphlings or is he going to abandon his quest to save his best friend and head of the guard? Decisions, decisions!!*

*And I'm going to do it again. I'm going to pick on the writers. They need to make up their mind is the Queen for saving the human race like her royal family wants and had decreed? Or does she want them decimated and enslaved like the Morphlings do. She seems to be flipping back and forth and back and forth!! OR are the writers crafty beyond belief and they are setting us up for something HUGE! Ah!! The possibilities. Alright enough of my blather. Share your thoughts!*

*Until next time EternallyEvers OUT!!*

*COMMENTS : **IFollowFlint:** I'm torn. I feel it might be a faction of the morphlings who are holding him. But I thought I heard a woman's voice and it WASN'T Zarina!*

> ***LochlanIsMine:** It has to be the Morphlings. They'll do anything to win the war. Taking Flint out of the equation gives them the upper hand.*

> *Response: **Morphing4Oberon:** I agree with you LIM it has to be the morphlings. I mean we know it's not the humans. They are too stupid to even know their existence is at risk. Who else could it be?*

\* \*

The next month flew by. Auditions had gone well. Abigail and Margot were really happy with their cast choices. And rehearsals were going like clockwork. Abigail was really proud how the cast had embraced the material and were each making it their own but working as a unit. She was sure it would be one of the best shows the school had done in a very long time. And Margot had taken to directing like a fish to water.

Margot came up to Abigail after English class. "Miss Reese, I have a question."

"What can I help you with?"

"Can we use your classroom after school today?"

"Who are we?"

"A couple of us from the show want to go over two scenes from the second act. But the auditorium is being used by the debate club. They have a match or meet or whatever it's called tonight. So they are rehearsing after school."

"How many of you?"

"It'll be me and four others."

"Sure, I can give you guys two hours."

Margot smiled, giving Abigail a happy little hop. "Thanks so much! I hope we aren't keeping you from something else. I know as our advisor you need to be there. We really appreciate it."

"Not at all, Margot. It's my pleasure. If you guys are taking the initiative to rehearse on your own, far be it from me to dampen that kind of enthusiasm."

When the impromptu rehearsal was over, Abigail headed to *Marcon's* for her weekly dinner with Tess. Tess was already there and she had ordered drinks for them that arrived just as Abigail sat down.

"Sorry, I'm late. I had a last minute rehearsal to attend."

"Sounds like the kids are really getting invested."

Abigail nodded. "I was really worried because so many of them wanted to do a musical, but they are full steam ahead. I couldn't be happier."

"And how is Chaucer going?"

"So much better!" Abigail practically squealed. "They are really moving through it. I knew they would like it once they got started."

"I think you need to take some of that credit. You are a really great teacher. You have a way with your students. They'll be sorry when you leave."

"Leave? I have no intentions of leaving. What would make you think that?"

"I just assumed with who you are dating that you would be making a move sometime in the near future?" Tess gave Abigail a sly smile.

Abigail shook her head and laughed. "Wow! Talk about jumping to conclusions.

Tess took a drink, shaking her head. "I'm not concluding, I'm deducing?"

Abigail raised an eyebrow. "Alright, deduce me. This should be good."

The server came and took their order before Tess continued. Once she was gone, Tess continued. "First, you and Liam had a strong connection from the word go. I actually wish I had been there to see it. I bet there were visible sparks, but I digress. Second, you guys talk every day! I mean who does that?! Even you and I don't talk every day."

Abigail smiled. Tess hadn't said anything that wasn't true. "Is that all you have?"

"I have one more fact that is completely indisputable."

"And that is?"

"That I have never seen you happier in the twenty years that I have known you than you are right now. And that right there is enough to prove my point." Tess gave a triumphant laugh.

Abigail couldn't dispute the truth. "You know, he invited me up to Canada to spend my spring break with him."

"Well! That is a new development that I can get behind. Dish please!"

"There is nothing to tell really. He asked me last night."

"And? Don't play games with me, woman! Are you going?"

"Of course I am!" Abigail laughed. "It'll be my first trip to Canada, I'm very excited."

"I'm sure you'll have a wonderful time. And I expect pictures! Especially if you can get some from the set!"

Abigail's face clouded over, she took a long sip of her amaretto sour. She waved the server over to get her another one. "I'm thinking about giving up my blog."

Tess almost spit out her lemon drop martini. A little dribbled out of the left side of her mouth. She quickly whipped it away. "I'm sorry, what?!"

Abigail started to play with the corner of the tablecloth. "I think I need to stop. I mean, Liam still doesn't know the truth. It feels wrong somehow now every time I write a new one. I feel like I'm betraying him or something?"

"Betraying him? That's ridiculous. What makes you feel like that? He isn't talking bad about his fans, is he?"

"No, no! It's nothing like that."

Tess sighed. "You haven't told him, have you?"

Abigail shook his head.

Tess took Abigail's hand. "Look, I understand that you want to tell him the truth and you seem to be struggling with it."

Abigail nodded.

"So tell him about the blog, and then immediately tell him why you hid it from him. The whole truth. If he is really the guy that I think he is, all will be fine."

Abigail looked at Tess. "And if it's not?"

Tess shrugged. "Then he's not really the guy for you, is he?"

"You make it all sound so simple." Abigail snickered.

Tess cocked her head to the side. "Isn't it?"

# CHAPTER FIFTEEN

———◆———◆———

A bigail tossed and turned all night. Even in her dreams she couldn't escape the memory.

*Abigail was so excited. Over the last two years she had paid her dues working at the Sci-Con event that was held every year at the convention center in New Haven. It was only thirty-five minutes from where she lived so her father had no problem dropping her off and picking her up. He had been to enough Soap Opera conventions since she was ten that when she got into the science fiction genre, he couldn't take it anymore. He was proud of his daughter. She was mature for her age and he trusted her enough to go it alone at the conventions that were close by. She wasn't allowed to go to any night events, but she didn't mind.*

*This year she was a guide to one of the stars appearing. Even though she was only seventeen, she had shown such maturity over* the past two years her supervisors thought she was up for the task. It really helped that she looked and acted older than she was. She had always been an old soul, or so her grandmother has told her.

Abigail had just touched her make-up before heading to the waiting pen to be introduced to her charge for the day. She was rounding a corner when she heard two voices. She slowed down because she recognized the voices. One was Ryan Motlen and the other was Courtney Whelan, two of the stars of **The Lost Continent.** The show was in its second season and had already been renewed for two more seasons by the network. It had a huge following since season one and it didn't seem to be losing momentum. The actors had become an overnight phenomenon and were gaining more and more fans with each episode. Abigail took a step forward but was blocked from their view by a bit of a corner and some plants. She could see them, but from the way they were standing, they couldn't see her.

"Don't get me wrong I love being on this show and the money I'm making is on point!" Courtney mentioned.

Ryan nodded. "Right? My agent just got me a pay bump for the next two seasons and let me tell you it's a sweet one!"

"Shit! I need to get my agent on that! If I have to keep smiling and laughing at all these freak fests plus all the work the show requires, I definitely want more money for the next two."

"I'm having a great time with the fans." Ryan laughed. It was a throaty laugh that gave Abigail a bit of a shiver.

"Ack! I'm all for having fans, I mean they are a great ego boost and all. But I did my time on a soap opera and those idiots *could never separate me from my character. Or worse the ones that could actually think they knew me! Like really? All they knew was whatever garbage I spewed out at an interview," Courtney scoffed.*

*"Ha! Interviews are my favorite. Give them a few bleeding heart tropes about your youth or early career and just watch the gifts start rolling in."*

*"What tropes? You grew up in an influential family and had everything you wanted including two very attentive parents, who are wonderful by the way. Your dad makes the best barbecue and your mom! Best cookies ever. You were one lucky kid!"*

*"You know that, and I know that. But the female fans who send me gifts even though I make more money in a year than they will in ten don't know that."*

*Courtney playfully hit Ryan. "You're so bad."*

*"Don't you know it!" Ryan grabbed Courtney up into a kiss. They stayed like that for a moment when Courtney broke away.*

*"Stop! You know the show would kill us if anyone found out about us yet."*

*Ryan took a step back. "Ugh, I hate that we have to keep this a secret."*

*Courtney touched his cheek. "Just until the end of the season. It's not that much longer."*

*He kissed her palm and let it go. "Come on, we need to get back to the pen room. Time to meet our handlers."*

*"Whoopee!" Courtney twirled her finger in the air. "I hope I don't get stuck with some super fan."*

Ryan laughed. "Don't you know my sweet, all the handlers are super fans. They just couldn't afford to buy tickets to see us. So now, they get to work for us for a day. So, try to be nice. And if you can't then nice be fake, otherwise the show will fine you."

"I think I'll go for the latter."

"Do your best. But you know it's the quiet ones that you have to watch out for. They're the ones with the blogs and all the fanfiction."

Ryan pulled out his phone. "Speaking of blogs you've got to see this one, it's called Continent Confessions. It's pretty racy at times, but has a good number of followers. Although it's clearly run by a teenage girl. She calls herself JakesMyEvery."

Courtney looked at the phone. "Her every what?"

"Her every sweet dream I suppose." Ryan chuckled.

"Gross!" Courtney laughed. "Look, look! She ends each blog post with a tagline - until we drift together again, JakesMyEvery OUT!"

"See, she clearly has a crush on me. I'm sure a hug and kiss from me would give her quite a thrill."

Courtney lightly punched his arm. "The only woman you can give any kind of intentional thrill to is me, and don't you forget it."

"Yes dear." Ryan gave Courtney a coy little smile and batted his eyes.

They both laughed as they wandered into the holding pen area.

Abigail couldn't believe what she had heard. Did everyone feel the same as they did? Probably not, but she was sure there were more *like them. More than she'd like to admit. She pulled herself together. She had a job to do, and whether or not she had a new taste of reality, she had a responsibility she wasn't about to renege on.*

*Head high and back straight, Abigail walked into the holding room and found her supervisor.*

*"Oh Abi, just in time. Let me introduce you to who you will be helping today." Mark led her over to Ryan Motlen. "Ryan, I would like you to meet Abi. She is one of our best workers. She'll be assisting you today."*

*Ryan grabbed her hand in his. "Well it's wonderful to meet you. We are going to have a great day. I've been looking forward to this event all month. So tell me about yourself."*

*All Abi could do was smile and say "Hi."*

*Mark looked at Abi to see if she was okay. Abi gave him a slight nod and smile. "It's nice to meet you, Mr. Motlen. I have your schedule for the day. It includes your breaks so please let me know if there is anything I can get for you.*

*"Well you can start by calling me Ryan, please."*

*"Okay, Ryan then."*

*Ryan looked at Mark. "So serious this one." He gave Abigail a smile.*

*"Oh she's a great employee. I'm sure once your day starts, you'll see." Mark nodded. "You should ask her about her blog. She writes one for your show. It's very entertaining."*

*"Oh really?" Ryan grinned. "I'd love to read it."*

Abigail could see Courtney out of the corner of her eyes. She was stifling a laugh and rolling her eyes at Ryan.

Unfortunately Ryan and Courtney had joint sessions all day except for one. So Abigail was forced to be close to Ryan as well as Courtney. Many times they whispered to each other or mouthed the words 'until we drift together again' and then snicker. Abigail silently fumed when they would mention in their panels how they thought fan blogs were awesome and how they loved to read them, and sometimes even commented under secret names. Abigail knew it was all a lie. She knew they were just making fun of the fans who had shown them nothing but love and devotion. Eventually she couldn't take it anymore.

Abigail and Ryan, along with Courtney and her handler, Beth, were walking down the hall from a session they had just finished to the break room for their twenty minute respite. A fan stopped them in the hall. Beth went to stop them but Courtney put her hand up signaling it was okay.

"Hi, I'm Nicole, I was just in your last panel. And you said you liked to read blogs." The nervous teen handed a piece of paper to Courtney. "Here is mine, maybe you guys can take a look sometime."

Courtney gave the girl a forced smile. "Of course! Ryan and I would love to! Right Ryan?"

Ryan moved next to Courtney giving Nicole a squeeze on the arm and a million dollar smile. "Absolutely, thanks so much. Maybe Court and I can check it out on our break."

*"Really?" Nicole was elated.*

*It broke Abigail's heart knowing how excited that girl was, over such a huge lie.*

*"They are lying to you Nicole. They won't look. And if they do, it will just be to make fun of you." Abigail's voice was low and tempered as she tried her best not to explode.*

*"Excuse me?" Courtney was offended.*

*Nicole looked confused. She looked back and forth between Courtney and Abigail. "What? Really? But then why did they say—"*

*"Because they are horrible liars!" Abigail shrieked.*

*Ryan reached for Abigail. "Abi, sweetie, I don't know why you are saying this but—"*

*Abigail slapped his hand away. "Because I heard you, both of you laughing and mocking your fans."*

*Ryan and Courtney looked at each other. Courtney swallowed hard while Ryan tried very hard not to look guilty. A crowd had begun to gather.*

*"I believed in you, we believed in you. Became engrossed in your character's world and in turn became fans of the actors who portrayed them. You know some people here have saved all year just to have the chance to be in the same room as you, get an autograph and maybe a picture if they've saved up enough. And all you can do is laugh at us, look down on us, and make hateful mean comments about us. You are the worst of the worst!"*

"*Listen here Abigail, you need to stop lying,*" Courtney huffed.

"*You're the liar, not me!*" Abigail shouted. She began pacing. "*Let's see Courtney, you think your fans are an ego boost for you, but otherwise you can't stand them. And you!*" She turned to Ryan, "*You try to get gifts from them even though how do you put it, you make ten times what they do?*"

Ryan tried to diffuse the situation. He smiled at Abigail, not reaching for her but leaning in a bit closer. "*Let's take this conversation into the break room, shall we? I'm sure it's just been a miscommunication.*"

*Miscommunication my ass!* Abigail thought to herself. It took everything within her not to push him away. "*Until we drift together again. It's what the two of you have been joking and snickering about all damn day! That's my blog asshole!*"

"*Continent Confession! I love that blog!*" Nicole chimed in.

"*You've been making fun of me ALL day! ALL day! And I've taken it because that's my job. But now you are lying to Nicole and I say enough! You are both disgusting, terrible human beings and I hope your characters both get killed off! You've ruined the show I love with your evilness and feelings of superiority. You are no better than any of us! You disgust me!*" She spat at their feet and walked away. A few fans that had gathered clapped in agreement before walking away themselves. No one noticed that Beth had filmed the entire incident. No one noticed until it was online later that night

Abigail gasped as she sat straight up in bed. She wiped the sweat off of her face. She got up to splash some water on her face. She took a long cold drink as well. She sighed. Her mind forced her to relive it over and over. Fifteen years had passed and yet here she was. How was she ever going to be able to tell Liam? *The Lost Continent* had run for another four years. Abigail had never watched another episode and shut down her blog when she got home that day. She also had never stepped foot in another fan event of any kind.

# CHAPTER SIXTEEN

*And That's All I Have To Say About That!*

*All Things EverMorph All the Time*

### UPDATE REMINDER

*H*ello my dear sweet Everrites and Morphlings. Surprise!! An unexpected, and super short blog just for you. Oh Yae! Oh Yae! Here is your official reminder of the grand contest that the Queen and her favorite son are putting forth to us, their loyal subjects. All entries must be postmarked no later than next Saturday, not this one coming up, but the next. So get those applications (is it an application they are asking for? I never checked- oops!) out there! Remember to go to The EverMorphs official website for all the rules and the proper way to enter. I wish the best of luck to you all and hope the Goddess of Nyla blesses one of you wonderful readers with the winning invitation!

Until the next toe curling, mouth dropping episode - be well!

Until next time EternallyEvers OUT!!

Comment - **BeatriceBabes:** *Thanks for the reminder! Updating a friend as I type!*

* * *

Margot felt only a little guilty for what she was doing. But she figured it was a long shot that they would win and if they did, Miss Reese would be secretly glad. And wasn't it better to ask for forgiveness than permission? As the president of the drama club, she felt it was her duty. Margot looked at the tape one more time to make sure she didn't need to do any more editing. Only a couple of the other drama club students had helped her, ones she knew she could trust. Her best friend Amanda, the vice president of the drama club, Jonathan, Sharon, a senior in the drama club, and Tara another club member. They had written a cute little script and acted it out. At the end, Margot had made a speech about how wonderful Miss Reese was, and all she did for them. And that this would be a treat not only for the rest of the club but their beloved teacher as well. Her and Amanda had sung a song at the end that Amanda had written. It was a parody of *The EverMorphs* theme song.

Margot had super imposed some photos of the drama club productions and playbills at the end when they were singing the song. To top it off and give them what she thought was a great advantage, she added the stickers that Miss Reese had given them over the term. Just the ones that were her secret references to the show. Margot had asked for extras and put them on the letter she sent with the video. She nodded, proud of herself for what she had done. She was going to take it to the post office before school started. It was the Friday before it was due, and she wanted to make sure it got postmarked before the deadline, it had snuck up on her sooner than she thought. She had even decorated the puffy package envelope. The address was clear, but it looked like an aquarium full of sharks. After all, they were the home of the blue sharks. After tomorrow the club's fate would be in the hands of the Goddess of Nyla.

* * *

Abigail sat at her desk waiting for her students to finish their last test before spring break. She had given them the option: a major test before spring break with no homework. Or no test, and a project due upon their return from spring break. They had voted and had unanimously chosen the former. One by one as they finished their test they came up and left it on her desk and took a donut. Abigail always plied them with sugar after a test.

"Five minutes left, people."

Andrew raised his hand.

"Yes Andrew?"

"So absolutely no homework over the break, right?"

Abigail smiled. "Yes Andrew, no homework over the break. However—"

There was an audible groan across the room as the last students brought up their test. Abigail got up and moved the panel on the chalkboard to reveal the details of their Canterbury project. "This is the project that you will be assigned the first day you get back. It will be due two weeks later. Now, if you want, you can start it on your vacation. There will be no extra points, early grading or special consideration given to those of you who decide to start this on their vacation. I just wanted you to have the option."

"So we really don't have to start this?" asked Tori.

Abigail nodded. "No you don't. You don't even need to write this down if you don't want to, I'll be giving this same information to you when you get back. But in the meantime, I have more donuts so please help yourself. What I really want to hear are any good plans you may have for the break."

"What about you, Miss Reese? Any big plans?" Margot asked with a sly smile on her face. She was pretty sure Miss Reese was dating Liam Caffney, but she had no solid proof. Not that she hadn't been digging for the dirt.

"I asked about *your* plans Margot, not mine." Abigail smiled.

"My family is going to Florida to visit my grandparents. On my dad's side, not the nasty ones from my mom's side. And we are also going to Harry Potter World."

"Now that sounds like some nice plans. And since you answered my question. I'll answer yours. I am indeed going away on vacation."

\* \* \*

Liam sat in his trailer. He knew the next scene but wanted to go over it one more time before he started shooting. He put some classical music on and closed his eyes. His lines moved like musical notes through his head as he listened. A knock on the door interrupted him. "Come in."

The door opened and Ted came in. "Hey, I have an official invitation for you."

"Oh really?"

"Well, it's not just for you."

Liam chuckled. "Okay, now you've piqued my interest."

Ted handed Liam a very fancy envelope. Liam raised an eye at him. "A little fancy for a poker invite, don't you think mate?"

"Ha-ha! It's Connie. She's way into decorating at the moment. Just open it."

Liam opened the envelope to find an invite to a dinner party. "Oh, isn't this lovely!"

"She's really hoping you and Abi can make it. Secretly I think she's dying to check her out. Make sure she passes her test of worthiness for you."

Liam leaned back in his chair. "Trust me, she will pass. We'd love to come."

"Great! My uncle will be there too. He's in town for a show. They are actually bringing his show back, but with an all new cast. They got most of the original cast back to send off the new younger generation into the series."

"Really?"

"He thinks it's a ridiculous concept and will get cancelled quickly. But if it doesn't, then it means some recurring work for him a couple of times a season."

"I guess retirement didn't suit him?"

Ted snorted. "Not even close! He's been teaching the entire time, but he can't stay away from a camera."

"But wasn't that show on like twenty years ago or something?"

"You know the saying - Everything old is new again."

"Is that really a saying?" Liam laughed.

Ted shrugged and started laughing.

"What was the name of the show he was on again?" Liam asked as he took a sip of his tea.

"It was called *The Lost Continent*."

There was a knock on the door. It opened and Piper, Liam's favorite PA, poked her head in. "Liam, they are ready for you on set." She looked over and saw Ted. "You too, Mr. Rendfell." She closed the door behind her.

"Mr. Rendfell?" Liam questioned.

Ted shrugged. "I don't think she likes me very much. But she keeps it professional."

"You know, if you asked her to call you Ted, she would. That's what I did."

"Oh really? You asked her to call you Ted?"

"Oh man! Was that a dad joke? It sounded like a dad joke. Is there something you and Connie need to tell me?" Liam laughed.

Ted laughed and rolled his eyes. "If there is, it's a surprise to you and me both! First marriage, and then a baby, maybe." Ted opened the door to the trailer. "Come on, last shot of the day."

"Ah! So you've been thinking about popping the question to Connie." Liam clapped his hands. "That's great man!" Liam followed him out.

Ted gave him a wink and shrugged his shoulders. "I plead the fifth."

Liam nodded. "Alright mate, change of topic, only one more day until Abi is here."

# CHAPTER SEVENTEEN

❖————❖

L iam met Abigail at the airport. He was waiting in the baggage claim area with a newsboy cap and sunglasses. He had his hair pulled back and a sign that read Miss Abigail Reese in a wonderful calligraphy. He greeted her with an English accent. "Are you Miss Reese? Miss Abigail Reese? My name is Giles and I'll be your driver for the duration of your stay. Welcome to Toronto."

Abigail giggled but played along. "Well, it's nice to meet you, Giles. I just need to grab my luggage and we can go, yes?"

"Allow me to grab your bag, madam. What does it look like?"

"Why thank you, Giles. It's a black suitcase with two big yellow daisies on it. The front of the suitcase is cloth and the flowers are embroidered on it."

"Oh, you mean like that one?" Liam pointed at a suitcase coming across on the conveyor belt.

"Yes! That's the one."

Liam went and grabbed the bag. He came back with her bag in hand and offered his arm to Abigail. "Shall we ma'am?"

Abigail nodded. "That would be lovely."

Liam dropped the act as soon as they got to his car. "How was your flight, love?"

"It was great. I slept most of the way."

"And what about Casseopia and Dipper? Were they mad you left them?"

"Oh, I gave them lots of lovies before I left, and they always have a good time with their Aunt Tess. She spoils them more than I do. How was work?"

"It was great. Another day of fighting evil fairies and saving the human race. You know, the usual."

"You know, I actually started watching the show. I wanted to see what you were doing."

Liam gave her a look. "Really now? You started right from what is it? Season four that's playing now?"

Abigail shook her head. "I started from season one. I found it streaming on one of the internet platforms. I think it was FlixArt."

"Ah yes, the internet is a wonderful thing. And because it's so wonderful, we don't get residuals from that."

"Do you want me to stop watching?"

"Would you if I asked you to?"

"Of course. But I don't know why you would want me to." Abigail thought she really needed to stop lying. She thought mentioning the show would help her ease into the truth she wanted to tell him this trip. She was firm on that. She had decided it was time to come clean and just let the chips fall where they may.

"I would never ask that of you." Liam winked. "Just wanted to see how much under my spell you truly are."

"Oh, I'm under a spell, am I?" Abigail moved her hand up his thigh and gave it a squeeze, letting it rest there.

Liam chuckled as he swallowed hard. "Careful now."

"Oh, I'm sorry, I'll move it." She moved her hand even closer to his crotch.

Liam let out a low groan. "Abi, I'm driving."

Abi gave his thigh a squeeze again. "Then keep your eyes on your road. And be careful." Liam gulped and tried to steady his breath. "I thought I'd cook for you tonight since you were so nice and cooked for me last time."

"Oh! What are you making?"

"I have some steak filets marinating and some twice baked sweet potatoes ready to pop in the oven and then I'll grill some asparagus with the steaks."

"That sounds delicious." Abigail gave Liam's thigh another squeeze. "How long can the steak marinate?"

Liam licked his lips and took a quick glance at Abigail. "Long enough."

Liam was kissing Abigail before he had the door locked. He had her pinned against the door as his tongue explored her mouth. She could feel his bulge growing against her the deeper he made his kisses. She moaned at the feeling. "I've missed you, and I can feel you missed me." She reached down to stroke the bulge through his pants before unzipping them and reaching her hand down to fully grasp the rod that was awaiting her touch. He groaned, thrusting his hips towards her hand. He kissed her a moment longer and then pulled away with a final kiss. He took her hand and led her to the bedroom.

"Stay right there, love." Liam went back to the front door and locked it. He went back to the bedroom to find Abigail exactly where she had left her. She was sitting on the end of the bed looking around his room. It was a comfortable room. A king size bed with a nice down quilt in a simple shade of green. There were four pillows on the bed. None were decorative. He had a long dresser opposite the bed and a large tv mounted above it. There was a wall of large windows that looked out onto the water. The opposite wall had some artwork framed and arranged nicely. Each piece was from a different artist, that much Abigail could tell.

Liam stood in the door frame for a few minutes just watching Abigail look around his room. He could feel himself falling in love with her. The thought scared him but also excited him. It had been a long time since he had felt like that. She caught him looking at her and smiled. She reached out her hands to him.

Liam kissed her and then started lifting up the top of her shirt. "May I?"

Abigail nodded and lifted her arms up. Liam lifted the shirt off of her and kissed her. He stood her up and kissed down her belly, stopping at her jeans. He unbuttoned them then slowly pulled down the zipper as he looked into her eyes. She took his hair out of the ponytail it was in and ran her fingers through it. Liam pulled down her jeans to the floor. Abigail gingerly stepped out of them. He turned her around, giving her soft kisses down her neck and back as he undid her bra. She cooed at the feeling. She could feel it was more than lust in his heart right now, and that made her tingle even more. Liam turned her around again and just looked at her. He ran his fingers from the top of her head down to her toes. He made swirls with his fingers and also tapped when he wanted to. He loved the way her skin felt under his hands. It was soft and supple. She had a few goose bumps and he looked up at her. "Are you cold?"

Abigail shook her head and huskily said, "No. Your touch just makes me quiver. I love the way your hands feel on me."

He smiled and kept touching her until he had worked his way back up to her head. He gently took her face in his hands and began kissing her again. First just the bottom lip then the top, then both. Abigail bit his lower lip, making him groan. He wrapped his arms under her arms and pulled her close to him, deepening the kisses as he did. It caught Abigail off guard and she sucked in her breath as she began to melt in his arms. He laid her on the bed and pulled her panties off. He loved watching her raise her hips to him to get them fully off. He could see she was glistening, just waiting for the touch of his tongue or his fingers or his throbbing cock. He licked his lips thinking which one he wanted to enter her first.

Liam moved her legs and he nestled himself between them. He began to let his tongue play with her breasts. She moaned as she felt his warm tongue against her hardening nipple. He slowly moved into her as she arched her back, yearning for his lips around her nipple.

Abigail gasped as she felt Liam's rock hard shaft enter her, filling her up fully. Her folds holding him deep within her. He smiled as he felt her walls around him, hot and wet, wanting him. They moved together like a current following the phases of the moon, waves of pleasure surging through them both, in sync with their moans and pleasure touches. Legs entangling and arms roaming and eventually entangling. In the end hands clasped together, forgetting everything around them except each other at this moment, finally climaxing one after the other. They were satiated and content lying in each other's arms.

Abigail played with one of Liam's curls. Just twirling and curling it between her fingers. Unable to erase the smile from her lips.

"You seem happy." Liam smiled as he gazed at Abigail's face.

She nodded. "You make me exceedingly happy. "

"Are you hungry?" Liam caressed her face and then began playing with one of her braids. "I still have those steaks marinating."

Before Abigail could answer, her stomach answered for her with a loud rumbling making them both laugh. Liam gave her several kisses before getting up. Abigail stared at his perfectly tight, round ass as he went to get his jeans.

"I can feel you staring at my ass." Liam laughed.

"It's a pretty fabulous one," Abigail stated.

Liam turned to her as he zipped up his jeans. "Do you want to help or stay here?"

Aoife meowed and jumped up on the bed. She walked over to Abigail and promptly began kneading her thigh before circling to make her spot. Abigail scooped the cat up in her arms giving it snuggles. "I think I'll stay here with Aoife for a bit. I'll join you as soon as she tells me how she likes living with you."

Liam went and gave the cat a scratch behind the ear and a kiss on the head. "Now Aoife, don't go telling Mommy all of Daddy's secrets, okay?"

Abigail looked at Liam, but said nothing, she just smiled as she felt her heart start to beat faster. Right at that moment she knew she was in love with him. She gave Liam a wink. "Us girls have to have our secrets. So why don't you go start those steaks Daddy, and we'll be right in."

Liam raised his eyebrow. He liked that she referred to him as Daddy when talking to his cat. But it was he who started it. After he said it, he was worried Abi would freak out. But apparently she hadn't, and had just gone with the flow. He had never met someone like her. He would have to thank Leenie for making him go to that fan event. He gave Abigail a kiss and grabbed a tee shirt before heading out to the kitchen and then the balcony where his grill was.

Abigail put her clothes back on. She put her hair in a ponytail and scooped Aoife up. "So tell me Aiofe, does your daddy talk about me when I'm not here?"

Aoife meowed in response. "Oh he does, does he? All good things I hope?" Aoife began to purr in her arms. "I love him, you know," she whispered in the cat's ear. "And I think he loves me too." Abigail giggled.

She watched Liam start up the grill and put the steaks on. He seemed to be enjoying himself. He was whistling as he worked. Abigail peeked her head out of the sliding glass door, kitten on her shoulder. "Want me to preheat the oven?"

Liam turned and smiled. "I see my two girls are getting along."

Abigail gave Aiofe a pet. "Always."

"If you could set it to four hundred that would be perfect, love."

Abigail turned to head to the stove. "I feel you staring at my ass." She laughed.

"It's a pretty fabulous ass." Liam chuckled.

# CHAPTER EIGHTEEN

------◆--------◆------

Liam's alarm went off earlier than either of them would have liked. Liam had pulled several strings and was able to get Abigail on set with him for the morning. She had to leave after the lunch break, but it was a compromise Liam was willing to accept.

Abigail groaned as she rolled over, putting the comforter over her head. She was an early bird, but even this was early for her. Liam pulled the cover off her head and gave her a kiss. "Up, up, we've got a busy morning."

"But it's my first day of vacation," Abigail whined.

"Well, if you don't want to go to the set with me today that's fine. I'll just see you when I get home tonight. Hopefully it won't be too late." Liam went to get out of bed.

Abigail grabbed his arm stopping him. "Wait, I get to go to the set with you? I can actually watch you film!?" She didn't try to hide her excitement.

Liam was pleased that she was excited. Even with her starting to watch the show, he wasn't sure how interested she would be in watching him work. And nothing big was happening today, no spoiling points, secret reveals, or cliff hangers. It's probably why the producers were pretty amenable to her being on set for the morning. "You'll have to sign an NDA and you'll need to leave after lunch. But yes, if you want to come watch you can."

Abigail jumped up and gave Liam a hug along with a big kiss. She looked him in the eye. "Do I have time to thank you properly for such a wonderful surprise?" She reached down and started stroking his cock.

Liam groaned and leaned into the tingles she was sending through his body. He bit his lip, debating on whether they had time. The things he wanted to do to her would require more time than they had. He knew that. But his mind went blank as he felt her hot breath on his growing staff, and then the wetness of her tongue as it wrapped itself around his tip gently sucking before engulfing all of him. His knees buckled and she grabbed his ass to help support him. She stayed like that, treating his hard cock like a big, long lollipop. Sucking all the great flavor out of it. As he was about to crest, he grabbed her head and thrust his hips, making her take him in even farther.

Abigail reacted by sucking and licking even harder making him explode and she drank all of him in. She smiled as she got out of the bed. "Want some eggs for breakfast? Maybe a little bacon and some nice sliced fruit?"

Liam was trying to catch his breath. He grabbed for Abigail, pulling her into a kiss. "You can't do that and just walk away. I want more." He kissed her again, cupping her ass and kneading it.

Abigail sucked his tongue for a minute before pulling away. "I'm so excited for today."

"I'm excited too, Abi." He kissed her again.

Abigail pulled away. "Not that kind of excited." Abigail giggled as Liam nuzzled her neck. It was becoming hard to resist him. "It can't be my fault that we are late today. I just wanted to give you a little thank you."

Abigail had a point and Liam knew it. "Alright Abi, you make a good point. But when we get home you are all mine." Liam gave her a deep kiss before heading to the kitchen. "I'll make breakfast, why don't you jump in the shower?"

They made it to set on time, they were actually a little early so Abigail could sign her non-disclosure agreement. Once everything was signed, Liam was able to give her a quick tour around the set before heading to his trailer to get his costume for the day before heading to the makeup trailer. Abigail followed Liam around, keeping very quiet. She smiled and nodded when she was introduced. She sat where Piper, the PA, told her it was safe to sit.

Liam and Ted walked over to her. Both had longer hair and fairy ears on. Liam also had wings that were closed and close to his back. Abigail's eyes became wide. It had been rumored that some of the Fae would have wings in either this season or the next season. So far there had been no sightings this season, but now Abigail had solid proof. And she couldn't tell a soul.

"Abi, this is my best mate Ted, he plays Flint on the show. And Ted this is Abi, the lovely woman I have been telling you about."

Ted walked up and gave Abigail a hug. "It's so nice to finally meet you. I have heard so many wonderful things. You know this lad is quite smitten with you."

"You can stop now, Ted!" Liam turned a little red in the cheeks.

"It's wonderful to meet you too, Ted. Liam speaks very highly of you."

"Lies, all of them I'm sure." Ted smiled. "Are you having a good time on set so far?"

Abigail couldn't hide her giddiness. "This has been amazing so far. I am loving every minute of it."

Ted gave Liam a look. Liam just shook his head. "Well, I hope we'll see you later this week. My Connie is dying to meet you."

"Connie?" Abigail looked at Liam.

"Yes, Connie is Ted's girlfriend. She invited us to dinner later this week."

"Oh! That would be nice." Abigail smiled.

---

---

"You didn't show her the invitation, did you, you big loser."

Liam shrugged. "I meant to, but she just got in last night and it slipped my mind."

Ted laughed and nodded his head. "Okay, I get it, I understand. It's the only acceptable reason. Just make sure you show up."

Liam crossed his chest with three fingers. "Scouts honor mate, we'll be there with bells on."

Piper came over interrupting their conversation. "Liam and Ted, you are requested on set for places please."

Ted nodded. "Abi, nice to meet you. Enjoy your day. We'll talk later. I can give you all the dirt on this one."

"No, no he can't." Liam gently punched his arm. He turned back to Abigail. "Enjoy the show." He gave her a quick kiss and went on set.

Abigail was in all her glory. She couldn't believe where she was sitting and what she was watching, it was like the ultimate dream. She watched and listened and absorbed everything she could. What amazed her the most was Liam. She of course knew he was a great actor, his performances were proof of that. But she had never seen him in person, and it was beyond magic. He had such a gift, and talent. She couldn't take her eyes off him. Every time they stopped to reset something or because a line had been fumbled, she looked around at everything trying to memorize it all. The marks, the props, the pieces of green screen that would be filled in during post-production, the other actors and how they all interacted together not only when they were acting but when the camera wasn't rolling.

Abigail was filled with love. Love for the show she had been a fan of for the last four years, love for Liam, and love for the process of it all. It filled something in her she didn't know needed filling.

For Abigail the morning passed quickly. They filmed until one and then broke for lunch for an hour. Liam took her back to his trailer for lunch. When they walked in, there was a table with candlelight set up with two very large grilled chicken salads and sparkling lemon water in wine glasses. There was also a vase with six roses in it. Two yellow, two red, one pink, and one white.

"Oh Liam, this is lovely! How on earth did you have time to do this?"

"Piper, the PA, is very good to me. I asked for her help, and she was more than happy to assist when I told her it was for you." He pulled out a chair for her.

They ate lunch and then made out on the couch for a bit like two high school teenagers before Liam had to walk Abigail to security to let her out. She took the roses with her.

"You have my keys, right? Car keys too?"

Abigail nodded as she held them up. "Please tell your producer thank you. I had a really amazing time."

Liam nodded. "I will. And I'll see you at home tonight? I should be home by seven. Ted will drop me off. If it's going to be later, I'll call you."

"Yes, and I will have dinner waiting for you. And something amazing for dessert."

Liam wrapped his arms around her. "Something more amazing than you?" He rubbed his nose against hers and then kissed her.

"You certainly know how to make me melt, Mr. Caffney."

Liam smiled. "I try my best." He kissed her one more time and squeezed her hand before heading back to set.

Abigail was on cloud nine going back to the apartment. She was greeted by Aoife who was very happy to have someone home during the day. She immediately curled up as best she could in the crook of Abigail's neck and began to purr. Abigail grabbed something to drink and her notebook. She went out on the balcony and started to write.

# CHAPTER NINETEEN

———

Abigail woke up in Liam's arms. Her body was used to getting up early. The sun was just beginning to stream through his curtains. He had a soft little snore that actually reminded her of Aoife's purr. She stifled a laugh as she gently kissed his lips and slipped out of bed. She went to the kitchen to put some coffee on. She stooped over, looking in the fridge for some eggs and cheese to whip up an omelette when she felt something hard against her ass as two arms wrapped around her.

"Good morning, love."

"I see you are up and awake." Abigail stood up.

"Aye, that I am." Liam kissed her neck and then began sucking on it. That one movement made Abigail go weak in the knees.

"Don't, don't make me drop the eggs," she gasped. Her voice became raspy the longer his lips lavished her neck.

"I have a big day planned for you." Liam spun her around and kissed her as he took the eggs and cheese from her and placed them on the counter to her right. He took her hand and led her back to the bedroom and leaned her back onto the bed. "And this is only the beginning." He kissed her several times before deepening the kiss. Abigail was up for whatever he had planned. But she did have a few tricks up her sleeve. As Liam was kissing her, she surprised him by flipping him over so that she was on top and he was under her. She pinned his hands above his head, much like he had done to her at her place. "My turn to show you a few things," Abigail purred as she lowered herself onto his stiff shaft.

He groaned watching her slide lower, taking him in. "God, you feel amazing," Liam whispered as she gyrated her hips.

She leaned down and kissed him, letting her tongue dance with his. They spent the morning making love as the sunlight streamed in through the window.

By mid-morning they were in Liam's car. "Where are we off to?" Abigail asked as she held his free hand as he drove.

"I thought we would go to the CN Tower. There is a beautiful view from the top and there is a restaurant where we can grab lunch before our next stop." He kissed her hand and smiled as he drove.

Baseball cap and sunglasses on, they headed to the top of the tower.

"The city is so beautiful!" Abigail was in awe. The view was as grand as the one from The Top of the Rock in New York City. She had to admit it was actually better since this view included the water. She closed her eyes and took a deep breath, letting the sun hit her face.

"Perfect day for the view, isn't it?" Liam asked as he grabbed her hand.

Abigail nodded "Let's take a picture."

Liam used his long arms to take several really good selfies of the two of them. They walked around a bit and Abigail did notice that people would nod at Liam or mention that they loved him on the show in passing. But no one stopped to ask for autographs or pictures. They kept a respectful distance while expressing their admiration. Abigail had to wonder if it was a Canadian thing or if it was because so many shows filmed there, the folks were used to seeing actors from their favorite shows all the time. After Abigail had gotten her fill of taking pictures and enjoying the views, Liam took her up one level to the restaurant. They enjoyed a lovely lunch where again several people gave Liam a nod or a wave. He was always gracious and would nod, wave, and wink back. Abigail was impressed with his kindness. It gave her hope that he would be understanding when she told him her secret.

The server came back with Liam's credit card. He signed for the meal, leaving a generous tip as always. "Are you ready for our next stop?" He helped Abigail out of her chair and took her hand as they headed out.

"Can I have a hint?" Abigail asked. She didn't want the day to end,

Liam shook his head. "Nope. But I think you will like it."

They drove for a while listening to the radio. Eventually they pulled down a road and Abigail saw where they were going. "The zoo!! I love zoos. Well, the ones that actually care for their animals properly."

Liam smiled at his animal loving girlfriend. "Then I think you'll really love this one."

Abigail was giddy as she practically jumped out of the car and quickly walked to the entrance. Liam just shook his head and laughed. He loved seeing Abi be so excited. For a brief moment, he wondered if their children would have her giddiness and pure joy. He shook the thought off quickly. It was too fast and too soon. But it was a nice daydream all the same. Liam caught up to Abigail at the ticket window. Abigail already had her wallet out, ready to pay for tickets.

Liam put his hand over her wallet. "Hold on. I already have something planned." He gave the ticket agent his name and she pulled out two tickets and programs.

"If you have a seat to the right, your tour guide will be right out, Mr. Caffney."

Abigail gave Liam a look. "Tour guide?"

Liam nodded.

"You got us a private tour of the zoo?"

Liam nodded again and smiled.

Abigail hugged him and gave him a kiss. "You are just full of surprises, aren't you Mr. Caffney?"

Liam pulled Abigail in for a long lingering kiss. "That I am love, that I am."

Their guide cleared his throat, breaking the two apart. "Mr. Caffney, hi, I'm Jeff. I'll be your tour guide this afternoon."

"Hi Jeff, please call me Liam and this is my girlfriend, Abi."

Abigail waved. "Hello."

Jeff just looked at Abigail and gave her an odd look before quickly recovering and giving her a smile. "Shall we get started?"

Abigail sighed as she followed behind Jeff and Liam. She was familiar with the look she was given. It was the typical *'wow you're fat and why does this good looking skinny guy have you as girlfriend? Couldn't he do any better?'* She would choose to ignore it. She was having too good of a day to let some close-minded idiot ruin it. She squared off her shoulders and held her head high as she caught up to Liam who seemed to be in a bit of a heated argument with Jeff.

"I'm sorry sir, but she just looks too heavy to do the zipline. We have weight limits, you know."

"I'm not debating that. I am, however, questioning your deduction that my girlfriend is simply too heavy. You have no idea what she weighs as you have not even bothered to ask her. Instead you are being a coward and talking to me about it."

"But you're the one who booked the activity sir."

"And *she* is the one you have the question about, Jeff. Do you have a problem with her, Jeff?"

Jeff looked over Liam's shoulder at Abigail as she approached and gulped. "No of course not I—"

Liam put his hand on Jeff's shoulder. "How about this, Jeff. Why don't you run along and get your manager for me? I'd like to have a word with them."

"I just, of course sir. I'll be right back."

Abigail watched Jeff scurry off. "Where is he going?"

"To get his manager."

"Liam, it's fine really, I'm used to people like him."

"Well, I'm not, and you shouldn't have to be." Liam could see Jeff and his manager approaching them. He gave Abigail's hand a squeeze. "I'll be right back, Abi.

Liam walked over to Jeff and his manager, a tall woman with a bun in her hair and glasses around her neck. She reminded Abigail of her principle. All that was missing was a pencil stuck somewhere in her hair, and her being black of course. Abigail watched as the interaction went down. If she was honest with herself, the sight made her cringe a little. But if she really thought about it, there was a similarity to her getting used to fans interrupting their time and him getting used to her being fat shamed or ostracized because of her weight. There was a learning curve for both of them.

Liam walked back to her with a smile on his face. "We will have a new guide shortly. And a new first stop."

"I appreciate what you did Liam, but you really didn't need to. I can handle myself."

Liam wrapped her in a hug. "I know but let me be your knight in shining armour just this once."

Abigail stroked his cheek and gave him a kiss. "Always."

A new guide named Mindy came over with a big smile on her face. "Hi Mr. Caffney! I'm Mindy and I'll be your guide." She shook his hand and then extended it to Abigail. "And you are?"

"I'm Abi, nice to meet you."

"The pleasure is all mine, Abi. So, I've been told ziplining is out, but are you two ready for the experience of a lifetime?" Mindy had more zeal than they thought was necessary, but they loved her enthusiasm.

"Before we begin, can I just say I am a huge fan of yours, Mr. Caffney!" Mindy looked over her shoulder to see if her boss was around. "I know I shouldn't fangirl out on you, but I just had to say something. You are my absolute favorite."

Liam smiled "Please call me Liam. And I am honored that you are my favorite. Would you like a picture?"

"Well, I really shouldn't—"

"Aw come now, we're friends and all." Liam put his arm around Mindy. "Now hand Abi your phone so we can capture this moment. I know you must have it in a back or side pocket."

Mindy blushed as she took her phone out of her back pocket and handed it to Abigail.

"Alright, get nice and close!"

Liam winked at Abi as he put both arms around Mindy and pulled her into a tight hug. Abigail took several pictures, the last was the best when Liam planted a kiss on Mindy's cheek. Her face was priceless and Abigail had caught it on camera. She handed Mindy back her camera.

"Thank you so much. Shall we get started?"

"We'll follow your lead," Liam said.

Abigail pulled this hand, holding him back as Mindy started walking towards their golf cart. "Did you book us to go ziplining?"

Liam nodded. "But Jeff seemed to have a problem with the idea, so I set something else up with Mindy. Something better." He kissed her, ending the conversation as he gently pulled Abigail to catch up with Mindy. She decided to let it go and enjoy the day with Liam.

Mindy gave them an amazing tour taking them to all the popular animal spots as well as some of her favorite less known hidden gems around the zoo. They traveled mostly by golf cart but walked when she took them to the back section where only employees were usually allowed. Abigail had a sneaky feeling they had carte blanche to go anywhere they wanted after Liam's little talk with the hospitality manager.

So far, feeding the giraffes has been Abigail's favorite part of the day. That was until they reached their last stop. Mindy pulled the cart around the back of the big cat enclosure. She took them through the back to a big empty room. It reminded Abigail of a training room of sorts. She could see some balls in the corner and there were blankets and a table that had some bins on them. Mindy led them over to a little sitting area that was off to the side but still in the middle of the room.

"Please have a seat here. I'll be right back." Mindy quickly left the room.

"Do you know what she's doing?"

Liam smiled and shrugged.

"You do know! Tell me!"

"All I'll say is that it's your last surprise of the day. But who knows what tomorrow holds?"

"You're going to spoil me the whole time I'm here, aren't you?"

"Absolutely! That way you'll want to come back sooner rather than later." Liam gave her a wink.

Mindy came back in with a zookeeper who was holding a lion cub. "Liam mentioned to my boss how much you loved animals. That you volunteer at a shelter. He thought you might want to give this little girl a nice cuddle. Her name is Nyla."

"Nyla, really?" Liam asked with a raised eyebrow.

The zookeeper nodded. "We had a contest on our website. Nyla was the overwhelming winner. Second was the name Beatrice."

Abigail let out a loud laugh. Clearly the zookeeper didn't get it. But Mindy did. Mindy shrugged. "I may have suggested a name or two to a few people who voted."

"It's perfect." Liam smiled as the zookeeper put the cub in his arms. He gave it a good hug before handing her off to Abigail.

He watched as pure joy came across Abigail's face. She cuddled the cub right to her face and heard it purr. Her eyes welled up with tears. "Hello little one. Aren't you a sight to behold?" Everyone else in the room ceased to exist as Abigail had a moment with the little Nyla. Liam took out his phone and snapped picture after picture and Abigail was completely oblivious. After ten minutes the zookeeper had to take Nyla back to her mother. It was hard for Abigail to let sweet Nyla go but she was so grateful for the experience.

"I hope you and Liam had a great tour today. I really enjoyed showing you around. I can take you back to the entrance."

"That would be lovely. Thank you, Mindy. You've been a great tour guide," Liam said as they headed back to the golf cart.

Once back at the entrance the three took a picture together. Once with Liam's phone and then another with Mindy's. Liam held out a tip for Mindy. "You made our day Mindy, thank you so much."

"Oh thank you, but I—"

Liam took the money, put it in Mindy's palm and folded her fingers over it. "I insist."

Mindy looked around to make sure there were no supervisors or managers around. "Thanks! And again it was great meeting you. Thank you for the pictures. And you too, Abi. I had a blast."

They walked back to the car swinging their arms. It had been a very very good day.

# CHAPTER TWENTY

---◆-------◆---

*And That's All I Have To Say About That!*

*All Things EverMorph All the Time*

## GONE FISHIN'

*A*lright you Everrites and Morphlings, this week's musings will be delayed a week. Sorry folks but even this Everrite needs to leave the land of the fairies every once in a while for a wonderful vacation with the mermaids! But never fear, I'll be back next week to discuss everything EverMorph from both episodes so get ready! Oh, and has anyone heard anything about who won the contest?

*Until next time EternallyEvers OUT!!*

*Comments:* **NylaKingidon4Ever:** *Have a great vacation!*

*Morphing4Oberon: Mermaids?! Where did you go?!*

*IdolofIsla: Mermaids rule! Aren't they actually a type of fairy? How come there are none in Nyla? Can't wait to hear where you went.*

*Response: IFollowFlint: Yup! They are! Maybe next season we'll see some!*

The next two days were much the same for Abigail and Liam, sensual morning sex followed by visiting different areas of the Toronto that Liam wanted to share with Abigail. He had surprises of some kind almost every day. Her week was going by so fast and her phone was quickly filling up with photos. She was excited to show them all to Tess when she returned home. She had so much to tell her. As usual, Abigail was up first. She gave Liam a kiss on the forehead and headed to the kitchen to start breakfast. She felt like making ricotta pancakes. She hoped he had all the ingredients.

She looked in the refrigerator and was very happy to find some fresh ricotta from the Marketplace they had gone to the day before. She had forgotten she had picked some up. Abigail was on her tiptoes reaching for a mixing bowl when she felt Liam and his hardness grab her from behind. It had become their usual fare that once awake, Liam would walk her back to bed for some morning nookie. And then they would start their day. Today seemed to be no different until it was.

Liam kissed Abigail's neck reaching his hands underneath her negligee so he could play with her breasts and nipples. "Good morning, love," he whispered in her ear before he licked it. "I had a great dream about you." He kissed down her neck. Letting his hands roam down her thighs and between her legs, slowly stroking her slit. Feeling it get wetter at every touch.

"Really?" Abigail gasped as he tweaked her nipple and bit her neck. "Tell me about it."

"Let me show you instead." He wedged his legs between hers and guided her back down so she was bent over the counter and entered her from behind.

Abigail grabbed at the counter as she moaned, "Yes, Liam, yes." She loved the way he felt inside her. He made her entire body hum and vibrate with each thrust. She bit her lip so as to not cry out.

Liam could tell she was holding back. "It's okay love, I have thick walls."

Abigail started to moan loudly which only set Liam off. He enjoyed making her moan, and the louder the better. He could feel his cock getting even harder as her moans grew. He quickened his thrust and she bent over even further, giving him more access. He pulled at her braids wrapping them around his hand. "That's right love, open up to me."

"I'm yours Liam, only yours," Abigail moaned.

"That's my good, good girl." Liam kissed and nipped at her back between thrusts. It wasn't long before he could feel her walls beginning to quiver and her moans turned to gasps. Her walls clamped down around his cock as she climaxed moaning his name. He released deep within her moments later. Both were out of breath but very happy.

Liam looked at the ingredients on the counter. "Oh! Were you going to make ricotta pancakes?"

"I was, but I got a little distracted." Abigail smiled. "Would you still like some?"

"Yes please." Liam batted his lush green eyes at her. "Shower with me first?" He leaned in giving her a long, sweet kiss.

She could feel her body begin to tingle again. She grabbed his ass thrusting towards her.

Liam laughed. "I'll take that as a yes." He grabbed her hand and ran with her into the bathroom.

Abigail eventually was able to make some ricotta pancakes which they ate with blueberries and some Canadian pure maple syrup. She was cleaning up the dishes when Liam came out of the living room with a picnic basket and began rooting through the pantry and refrigerator.

"Are we going on a picnic today?"

"Yes! There is a special spot in High Park I want to take you to. I get some of my best meditation done there. You should bring a notebook. You might get inspired."

Abigail couldn't help but smile. Liam was really encouraging her to write more. She had surprised herself with how much she had written on this trip already. "I'll bring my notebook if you bring your camera. You never know what might inspire *you*."

Liam kissed her cheek as he playfully smacked her ass. "I'm pretty sure I know what my inspiration will be today." He finished packing the basket while Abigail finished cleaning up and getting ready. Thirty minutes later they were on their way to High Park. The parking lot was about half full by the time they got there. Abigail was a little worried it might be crowded. She didn't know how big the park actually was.

Abigail had no need to worry, the park was huge. She let Liam lead the way to his favorite spot. It was pretty secluded in comparison to many of the other wide open spaces in the park. This section had a lot of trees clumped together almost forming a grove of sorts with little pocket inlets. Some had people in them lounging about. Others had no one but the sun and some squirrels. Liam seemed to have a favorite grove set back a little farther from the others. No one was there. He laid out the big blanket he had brought along with two pillows that Abigail had never seen. He then rooted around for some drinks.

"Where did those come from? Abigail asked as she pointed to the pillows.

"Ah! Those are my park pillows. I keep them in my car at all times."

"You have park pillows? No decorative pillows on your bed, but park pillows in your car." She laughed.

"Of course! Doesn't everybody?" He winked. He handed her a drink and sat down.

Abigail followed, sitting next to him. "This place really is beautiful, thank you for bringing me here."

Liam began playing with Abigail's braids. He enjoyed the way they felt running through his fingers. "Are you having a good trip, Abi?"

Abigail closed her eyes, nodding. "I'm having a wonderful time. It makes me dream."

"Dream about what?"

Abigail looked in his eyes "Traveling the world with you. Seeing places I've never seen, never been to, and sharing that all with you."

"Should we quit our jobs and travel the world?"

Abigail laughed. "I was thinking something a little less drastic. Maybe after your next season and at the end of my school year, we can spend the summer together? They almost lineup, right?"

"That sounds lovely." Liam leaned in, giving her a kiss.

"Maybe start in Ireland and go from there?"

Liam pulled her up into his arms and kissed her, pressing his somewhat coarse lips against her petal soft ones. He looked into her eyes. "I love you." He kissed her again.

Abigail melted into the kiss, reaching to hold his hand. "I love you too."

Liam leaned against a tree and Abigail nestled into his arms. She sighed, feeling very content. This feeling is what she had wanted her whole life for and didn't know she had been holding her breath waiting for it to arrive.

They spent the afternoon in the park. Abigail got some writing done. Liam took out his camera and got what he thought were some great nature shots. They shared a brief nap lulled to sleep by the breeze from the trees. And munched on the treats Liam had packed in the basket. The sun was beginning to set by the time they started backing up.

"We have dinner at my friend Ted's house so we should start to head out. I want to shower and change before we go."

"Me too," Abigail agreed. Abigail stood and started collecting their belongings.

Liam pulled her into a hug. "Shower together?" he asked as he kissed her.

Abigail twirled her way out of his arms. "If we do that, we'll be late and you know it, so no."

Liam pretended to pout, sticking out his lower lip. Abigail took his face in her hands and gave him a kiss. "I'll make it up to you when we get home. I promise."

Liam couldn't help but smile. "It's home now, is it?"

"Maybe." Abigail winked and headed back down the path to the car.

# CHAPTER TWENTY-ONE

———◆———

Abigail looked at herself in Liam's full length mirror. She had already changed her outfit twice and was debating on trying one more outfit when Liam walked in. He looked amazing in his jeans and button down maroon shirt. The color played well with his eyes making them even greener.

"You look lovely Abi."

Abigail turned slowly one more time. "Are you sure? I can change into something else."

"We aren't going to meet the queen, just dinner with friends," Liam joked. He saw the look of concern on Abigail's face. "Have I mentioned you look gorgeous?" Her gray off the shoulder sweater hugged her in all the right places and her black jeans were a deep black so it was a lovely contrast. The scoop neckline showed off the necklace Liam had given her very nicely. Her black boots finished off the look nicely.

Liam was right, she did look gorgeous. "Okay, I think I'm ready. Wait! Just need some lipstick." She ran back into the bathroom to get her favorite lipstick out of her makeup bag. She applied it while looking in the bathroom mirror, puckering her lips and giving herself a wink. Now she was truly ready. Liam held the door open for her, giving her a peck on the cheek as they headed out.

Abigail looked out the window as they drove. "Ted lives in the suburbs?"

"Yes, he and his girlfriend bought it about a year and a half ago. You're going to love Connie. I have a feeling the two of you are going to get along really well. The show brought them together, you know?"

Abigail just nodded. Now that Liam knew she had started watching the show, she felt it would be fine to make a comment about it. "He does a good job on the show. You two work well together. At least that's what comes across on screen."

Liam reached for her hand and gave it a squeeze. "Thanks, love. We have a good time together, hit it off right away."

As they pulled into the driveway Ted opened the door and waved. "Welcome friends!"

Liam and Abigail got out of the car and headed up the walk. Liam and Ted shared the standard bro hug. Then Ted reached out and pulled Abigail into a hug. "Abi! It's grand to see you again. This guy just wouldn't shut up about you after you left the set the other day!"

Abigail returned the hug. "Well, I hope it's all good."

"Oh yes! But not too good!" Ted winked.

"Ted! Stop standing in the doorway and invite them in!" Connie called from the living room. She had set out a nice spread of hors d'oeuvres.

They came into the living room and sat down. "Connie, this is the infamous Abi," Ted introduced her.

"It's so nice to meet you." She shook Abigail's hand.

"So I'm infamous now?" Abigail gave Liam a look. He just shrugged and smiled

"Don't worry, it's a good thing." Connie smiled. "Especially with this one over here. What can I get you to drink? Wine? I've got red and white."

"I'd love some red." Abigail could tell she would like Connie.

"I'll take red too please." Liam put his arm around Abigail.

"I think it'll be red all around, hun." Ted nodded.

"No problem, Abi, would you mind helping me?" Connie asked.

"Of course not." Abigail stood up and followed Connie into the kitchen.

"Can you get the wine opener? It's in the drawer on your left," Connie asked as she pulled the wine glasses out of the cabinet.

Abigail found it quickly and handed it to Connie. "You have a lovely kitchen. I wish mine was this nice, I wish mine was this size!"

"Apartment kitchen?"

Abigail nodded. "How did you know?"

"I used to wish the same thing until we got this house."

"Oh, so you live here year round? Not just when they are filming?"

Connie nodded. "I'm a native. I met Ted here on his last show. I actually helped him find his apartment while filming."

"Real estate agent?" Abigail asked.

"Yup!" Connie opened the wine, handing the cork to Abigail. "I helped Ted find his place like I mentioned and then helped a bunch of his other cast mates. That show only lasted a season and a half. They cancelled it mid-season. When he came back for *EverMorphs,* he called me again and brought half of his cast with him. I somehow became the unofficial realtor of *The EverMorphs.* I'm not complaining, mind you. It's been quite the gift. And I got a great possible husband out of the deal."

"Really? Are you expecting a ring soon?"

Connie smiled. "I'd like to think so. I'm kind of getting a feeling off of Teddy lately. He'll deny it of course. But a woman knows."

"I'm so happy for you! That's exciting!"

"What's exciting?" Ted asked as he came in for more shrimp cocktail sauce.

Abigail looked at Connie and gave a slight nod. "My first trip to Toronto. It's all been so exciting."

Ted looked back and forth between the two women. For some reason, he didn't believe them. He turned his head towards the living room. "Liam! I think our girls are getting along too well! This could be a problem." He gave a wink to Connie. Abigail just shook her head. Another winker. Was everyone on the show winkers? Connie handed Abigail two glasses, she grabbed the other two, and the three headed back into the living room.

"What's this I hear? Are the ladies getting into trouble already?"

Abigail gave Liam a glass of wine. "Just telling secrets."

"Ack! Teddy, we're doomed! They are already sharing secrets!" Liam joked.

"And they are *really* juicy!" Connie teased.

"Abi! Did you tell her about the time we did the thing and how it made you—"

Abigail gave Liam's arm a playful slap. "Oh my god no! Stop talking!"

They all started to laugh.

"And on that note I think dinner is ready. Ted, show them to the dining room and I'll get the food." Connie left to get the meal out of the oven.

"Yes dear," Ted replied in a very sing-song voice. He showed them into the dining room. Connie had made beautiful place cards in the shape of different kinds of trees. Each one had individual leaves on the branches and their names were spelled out in the roots.

Liam gave a long whistle as he picked it up and looked at the details. "Teddy, you weren't kidding when she said she was in a decorating mood."

Abigail nodded in agreement. "These are gorgeous." She noticed the extra place setting, but there was no tree name for it. "Are we waiting on someone?"

"Oh, my uncle was supposed to join us. He's in town on business but got held up. He might be here for dessert."

Connie came in before Abigail could say anything else and put a large roast beef platter on the table. It was surrounded by roasted carrots and potatoes. "Dinner is served. Oops! Almost forgot the rolls. I'll be right back." Connie dashed back into the kitchen and was back in a moment with a dish of hot rolls. Abigail could see the steam rolling off of them. "Bon Appetit!" Connie took her seat. "Ted, will you do the honors?"

Ted cut up the roast beef as everyone handed them their plates for him to put some slices on. The rest of the food was passed around and everyone took what they wanted. For a few minutes all you could hear was the sound of silverware on plates and people enjoying their food.

"This is just delicious, Connie. I want this recipe please."

"Thank you. I'd be happy to share it with you. So Abi, tell me, how did you meet Liam?"

Abigail took a sip of her wine. "I would have thought he told you by now."

Connie nodded. "Oh, he did, but you know men, they never give good details."

"Hey, I take offense."

Abigail reached over and squeezed his hand. "Well, to be honest, my boss foisted Liam on me."

"Foisted?" Connie cocked her head to the side. "Do tell, I want details."

"As you may or may not know, I volunteer at an animal shelter once a month," Abigail started.

"Ah! So that's where he got the kitten from!"

Abigail nodded. "Yes, for some reason Liam agreed to help us out with our annual adoption and fundraising event. In the past we had celebrities come in and help raise money but no one of Liam's status before.

Liam smiled. "Did you hear that Ted, I'm of a certain status."

"Don't let your head swell mate. I'm still before you on the call sheet."

"Ouch! Right through the heart man!"

"Anyway, my boss Steve didn't want to team him up with one of our younger volunteers because he was afraid they would go fan crazy, and not be able to accomplish the task at hand."

"Hmm, you make fan sound like a four letter word," Connie noted.

"So," Liam interrupted, "they placed me with a seasoned professional. And the rest is history."

"A non-fan, interesting," Connie commented.

"Is it really that interesting? I mean most fans are-"

"Careful, love" Liam interjected. "Connie is a fan."

"Really?" That made Abigail feel much better. "You're an *EverMorph* fan?"

"Not just *EverMorph*. I was a fan of Ted before he even got that job. I loved him way back when he was on *Space Riders*."

Ted groaned. "An experience I wish I could forget, but someone owns the box set!"

"You bet your sweet bippy I do! It's even signed."

"Sorry Connie, Teddy's signature doesn't count." Liam laughed.

"Oh no, I have the entire cast, not just my Teddy." Connie smiled. It was a great accomplishment for her. Connie was proud to be a fan and it fascinated Abigail. "Dessert anyone? I made strawberry shortcake." Connie smiled as she got up and started to clear the plates.

"Let me help you, Connie." Abigail offered.

"Scotch?" Ted asked Liam

Liam nodded. "After you." They headed back to the living room.

In the kitchen Abigail began to probe Connie a little more. "So you were always a fan of Ted's work? Did that worry you at all about what he would think of you?"

"What do you mean?"

"Sometimes fans don't have the best reputation. I was wondering if it made Ted hesitant to get to know you. Or you know him?"

Connie thought about it for a moment. "I don't really think so. It's not like we met at a fan convention or anything. I was just the lucky realtor who was in the office when he walked in."

"So how did he know you were a fan?"

"Oh I told him. Once I had arranged his apartment, and the lease was signed, I told him and then asked him out." Connie smiled.

"And he was just like sure?" Abigail was astonished.

Connie laughed. "Oh god no! He was hesitant at first. So we just had coffee, and then another coffee, and then a walk, and then lunch, and so on and so on. Eventually we got to where we are now."

"So he was cautious because you were a fan, are a fan." It confirmed Abigail's beliefs on the matter.

Connie shrugged. "Maybe. But now, I think he thinks it's cute that I'm a fan of him and his work. Actually I even have a username dedicated to him."

"You mean like for your email or something?" Abigail inquired.

Connie reached for her phone. "Let me show you something." Connie pulled up a blog page. "I follow Ted's current show with a bunch of other fans. We comment and speculate on characters. It's a lot of fun. You make up a name to go with your profile. Usually it relates to the show, I guess you could use your own name if you wanted to. But I don't know anyone that does. I go by *IFollowFlint*. This particular show blog is run by *EternallyEvers*."

Abigail did her best not to show any emotion. "May I take a look?"

"Sure." Connie handed her phone to Abigail. She scrolled through it. She took a deep breath and let it out slowly trying not to panic. Maybe her first step could be to confide in Connie. She knew she had just met her, but if anyone would understand, Abigail thought it would be Connie.

"She's actually quite funny and very insightful about the show. You should make a profile and follow her! We could have some great fun."

Abigail gave Connie her phone back. "Connie, can I tell you something? But you have to promise not to tell Liam or Ted."

Connie thought about it for a moment. She knew that Abigail would be around for a while. She saw the way Liam lit up around her, talked about her when she wasn't there. And she had been there for the entire Monica debacle. She was so happy that Liam had some light and love back in his life, and she would do anything to help preserve that. If a secret could derail that, she wasn't sure she wanted to be the keeper of it. "I don't know Abi, I can't keep—"

"I'm *EtertnallyEvers*, the blog is mine!" Abigail blurted out.

"Blog! Do people still do those? Who has a blog? What's an *EternallyEvers*?" A tall man who resembled Ted in the eyes came into the kitchen. "I heard there was some strawberry shortcake in here."

"Uncle Ryan! I'm so glad you made it!" Connie gave Ryan a big hug. "I'd like you to meet Liam's girlfriend, Abi. Abi, this is Ted's uncle, Ryan Motlen."

Ryan stuck out his hand and gave Abigail his million dollar smile. "Have we met before?"

# CHAPTER TWENTY-TWO

L iam and Ted came into the kitchen.

"See Teddy, I told you the party was in here."

"We were just coming out with dessert." Abigail tried to pull herself together.

"I think they were telling more secrets. What do you think, Liam?" Ted jokes.

Liam nodded. "Trouble, with a capital T."

"Uncle Ryan, I see you met Abi?"

Ryan nodded. "Yes, as a matter of fact I was just asking her if we had met before." Ryan took a good look at her. "You just look so familiar to me, but I can't place you. Could I have met you at a fan event?"

"Not my Abi, she's not much for fandoms." Liam put his arm around her, kissing the side of her head.

Abigail moved into him. She needed to feel safe. She couldn't believe who was standing in front of her. The man who helped make *fan* a four letter word for her. The man who had shattered her at seventeen was Ted's uncle. "May I use your restroom please?"

"Sure, it's down the hall to your left." Connie pointed it out.

Abigail nodded. "Excuse me please." Abigail quickly walked down the hallway, and gently closed the bathroom door behind her. She took several deep breaths and ran some cold water over her hands, hoping it would help calm her nerves. She looked in the mirror. "The past is the past. You leave Ryan Motlen there. You can do this. And the minute you get home, you sit down and tell Liam everything." She took a few more minutes to collect herself. Gave a final nod to the mirror, put a smile on her face and headed out of the bathroom. She heard voices in the living room and headed in that direction.

"They say everything lasts forever on the internet, no matter how you try to delete it," Ryan confirmed. "I knew she was familiar, and it was gonna gnaw at my bones until I figured it out." He looked up and saw Abigail staring at them all as they huddled around Ted's laptop. Ryan turned the laptop around to show Abigail something she hadn't seen in fifteen years. It was the video of her outburst at Sci-Con she had participated in. It was old and a little fuzzy but there was no doubt it was her. She couldn't move or speak.

Ryan looked up at Abigail. "I owe you an apology, Abi. I was a selfish, self-absorbed son of a bitch back then. Way too big for my britches, and very unappreciative." Ryan shook his head and chuckled. "I actually got in a hot bit of trouble for that and so did my castmate if I recall! And some not too pretty hefty fines from the show. It was an eye opener for sure."

Abigail looked at Liam. He had a look on his face she had never seen, and it wasn't a good one.

Ryan continued, oblivious to the tension that was building in the room. "Let me make it up to you. It was a shame that you took your blog down after that. I know because I checked but what little I did read that day was really quite brilliant. Had to be to stick in this old noodle for so long. Maybe with the reboot of the show, you could take up the mantle again. It would be great PR for the show. And now that I have an inside track to you, I'm sure we could make something real good together."

Abigail went to sit down, but not next to Liam. She couldn't be that close to him right now. "Well, I-"

"You really were a die-hard *Lost Continent* fan. What about *The EverMorphs*? Do you have a blog for that too? Let's take a look." Ryan went back to look at the laptop.

Ted gently closed it, shaking his head. He got up to put it in the study where it belonged.

"Hey, Uncle Ryan, how about we skip that and have some dessert? Would anyone like coffee or tea to go with theirs? The whip cream is homemade." Connie started to hand out plates of dessert.

Ted came back into the room and looked at Liam. "Hey mate, will you help me get some more coffee and tea? I can't handle all of it without breaking something. And Connie will kill me if it's one of her favorite mugs or god forbid a teacup." He pretended to swoon.

Liam nodded as he got up. He turned to Connie. "Fear not, Connie. I'll make sure your cupware stays intact." He bowed and headed into the kitchen.

Ted already had the tea kettle on and the coffee brewing. He pulled out a chair for Liam to sit. "How are you doing there?"

Liam shrugged and shook his head. "She lied."

"Did she though? I mean that was fifteen years ago. She wasn't even an adult then. And trust me, from the stories my mom told me about my uncle back in the day, he and his co-stars weren't the nicest to their fans. Maybe get the full story before you make a judgement call."

Liam grabbed the teacups Ted handed him. "I don't know man, I think it's the lying more than the being a fan thing. You know the lies and deceptions I went through with Bianca, always the lies man."

"This is a lot I know, so maybe put it on the back burner for now and let's just have dessert and enjoy each other's company."

Liam nodded. "You're right. You're right. And now is not the time for it. Now is the time for tea."

"And coffee!" Ted held up the coffee mugs.

They walked back into the living room to find Ryan telling tales of his glory days on *Lost Continent*. Connie was being gracious and so was Abigail, but she looked like she was going to be sick. "And I'll be here filming a couple of episodes shortly after your men return to the set of *EverMorphs*! It'll be great!" Ryan smiled.

"It will be nice to see you more, Uncle Ryan."

"I'm hoping your girl here will help me find the perfect bachelor pad when the time comes. No hotel for me. I want my space."

Connie nodded. "Of course Uncle Ryan, not a problem."

Dessert continued to be awkward as both Abigail and Liam were having trouble keeping up their end of the conversations. Connie tried her best, knowing the shit was going to hit the fan eventually. She just hoped it would wait until after the evening was over.

Ryan could feel the tension, but he had no idea what for. He felt it was his duty to liven things up a bit. "So, how is everything going at *EverMorphs*? Only two more episodes to film right?"

Ted nodded. "Two more then a nice break until next season."

"What? No project in between? Connie, you're not turning my nephew into a slacker, are you?"

"Hey! Watch it, Uncle! I'm choosing not to do anything this break. I have some other plans that shall not be talked about at the moment."

Ryan shrugged. "I'll say no more." He pulled out his phone, looking for something.

"Ted told me you visited the set earlier in the week. Did you have a good time? Meet anybody?" Connie asked.

Abigail nodded as she finished her bite of strawberry shortcake. "Yes, I mean I didn't get to see much and I had to sign an NDA, but it was exciting watching Liam while he filmed. I wasn't even paying attention to the storyline. I was just watching everyone perform. It was wonderful, almost magical."

Ryan chuckled, "Sounds like a true fan to me. Liam, do you know what an EternallyEvers is?"

Liam shook his head. "I have no idea what that is."

"The ladies were talking about it when I came in. Apparently, your lovely girl is one."

"Uncle Ryan, you misunderstood what we were talking about." Connie tried to defuse the situation before it got any worse.

Liam looked at Abigail. "Do you know what he is talking about?"

Before Abigail could think of something to say, Ryan handed Liam his phone. "See this is Eternally Evers, or at least the person who runs what looks like a website blog all about your show! It's called *And That's All I Have to Say About That.*" Ryan turned to Abigail and smiled. "So you do have another blog. That's terrific. It means you haven't gotten rusty. We really do need to have a talk about you doing one for the reboot. I'm sure there would be a nice salary in it for you."

Abigail was dumbfounded. So she just remained silent.

"Sorry Ryan, this isn't Abi's blog. She doesn't have one." Liam grabbed her hands and gave it a reassuring squeeze.

"Huh, I could have sworn I heard her tell Connie that she was Eternally Evers." He turned to Connie. "Isn't that what she said to you, Connie?"

Connie had a bad poker face. She shook her head, but her facial expression clearly said yes. "As I said, you misunderstood. We were talking about a fan site, and fans in general, that's all."

Ryan looked back and forth between the ladies; eventually he shrugged and took a sip of his coffee. "Oh well, I guess I was wrong. It's been known to happen from time to time." He chuckled as he put his phone away and took a bite of shortcake.

The whole time this conversation had been going on Liam had been scrolling through the blog *And That's All I Have To Say About That! All Things EverMorph All the Time.* He had a feeling in his gut he didn't like. He prayed he was wrong. He wanted to believe Abi wouldn't lie about something this big. But he couldn't shake the feeling that his bubble was bursting. Liam gave a fake yawn. "I'm so sorry but I'm beat, and tomorrow is Abi's last full day, so I have one last big surprise planned for her."

Abigail stood up. "I had a wonderful time. I hope we get to spend more time together." She gave Connie and Ted a hug. "And thank you for the apology, Ryan." Abigail grabbed her purse and headed to the door.

Liam said his goodbyes and followed her out.

# CHAPTER TWENTY -THREE

The ride home was quiet. Halfway before they got back to Liam's apartment, he broke the silence. "Are you EterntallyEvers? Is that your blog? Are you a fan of the show? Of me?" He couldn't look at Abigail when he asked. He kept his eyes glued to the road.

Abigail turned to Liam, she saw the strained look on his face. She thought for a brief moment about lying to him, but she had promised herself she would tell him the truth. But the look on his face made her resolve soften a bit. She took a deep breath, not taking her eyes off of him. "Yes, it's my blog. I am EterntallyEvers."

Liam swallowed hard. A million thoughts went through his mind. He was angry and hurt and had so many questions.

Most of all he felt betrayed and deceived. So he stayed silent, unsure if Abigail would even tell him the truth at this point.

"I'd like to explain it all to you if you'll let me." Abigail tried not to cry. "I didn't mean to lie, I just didn't want the stigma that went with being a fan of the show, of you. And honestly, I never thought what happened between us would actually happen. I just thought we would have a great time at the shelter, that would be the end of it and I would have a happy memory. I never imagined any of this. And then we had feelings, I felt like it was too late to tell you about my blog and have you understand, so I just omitted it." Abigail took a short breath and kept going. "I was planning on telling you everything on this trip I swear. Ryan just beat me to it. I'm not some crazy stalker fan, I know the difference between you and your characters, I never meant to take you for granted or deceive you. I just, I just didn't."

Liam kept both hands on the wheel, not even giving Abigail a side glance. She waited for him to say something. He kept quiet and the silence was like a knife to her heart.

"Say something Liam, please. Ask me anything, I promise to give you an honest answer."

Liam gave her a quick look before concentrating on the road again. He reached his hand over and turned on the radio. He had nothing to say.

Abigail turned and looked out the window, finally letting the tears silently fall.

Liam opened the door for her, letting her enter his apartment first. He immediately went to the kitchen to pour two glasses of wine. Aoife wound herself between his legs and purred. He picked her up cuddling her for a moment before making sure she had food and water. Once she was settled, he entered his living room. Abigail was sitting straight up on the couch clasping her hands together and trying to keep her breathing even.

Liam handed a glass of wine to Abigail. She gratefully took it.

"So you knew who I was right from the start. You knew all about *The EverMorphs*. You mentioned seeing *Keys*. Have you seen anything else?"

Abigail nodded. "I've seen the majority of your movies and television appearances. You truly are a talented actor."

Liam sucked down half his glass. "Thank you. Are you in love with me, or who you perceive as the celebrity me?"

Abigail turned, grasping his hand in hers, looking directly in his eyes. "I love you, Liam Matthew Caffney. I love your kindness and your humor, your compassion, and your intelligence. I love your eye for photography and how you bring the natural beauty out in every image. I love how you treat others, and the warmth in your heart. I love how you love me and make me laugh. And yes, I love your talent. But that is only such a small part of all that encompasses who you are. Please believe me when I say there are no words for how sorry I am that I wasn't completely upfront with you from the beginning."

Liam kissed her hand as he leaned his cheek against it. He closed his eyes for a moment. And just let himself breathe. He hadn't realized just how long he had been holding his breath as Abigail poured her soul out to him. "I believe you."

Abigail let out a sigh of relief. "You deserve to know the whole story about that video and why I feel the way I do about being a fan, and why I hid it from you." She looked down as she gulped the remainder of her wine.

Liam shook his head. "I saw enough to get the gist and I don't think you are really ready to share that yet. And I have a sneaky suspicion Ted's uncle has something to do with it and I don't know if I want that whole story at the moment. But is there anything else I should know? You aren't hiding anything else back are you? I can't take the lies, Abi. I had enough of that in my last relationship. I'm not doing that again, ever!"

"I promise there is nothing else."

Liam drew Abigail to him and kissed her. "Only honesty from now on, okay? I can't be with someone who lies to me."

"I promise, only honesty." She kissed him, wrapping her arms around him. She didn't want to let go. They just stayed like that until Liam's phone rang.

Begrudgingly he released himself from Abigail's arms to answer it. He got up and walked away to take the call. It was the studio. A moment later he came back in, still on the phone and just stared at Abigail as he talked. "Yes, so you have the winner of the contest. You want me to see their show.

Yes, I can do that. Okay, what school am I going to again? It's in Connecticut? It's Odyssey High, home of the fighting blue sharks? And can you tell me what put them over the top? Oh, their teacher makes homemade stickers for her students about *The EverMorphs*? Great, just email everything and I'll be there with bells on. Wouldn't want to disappoint my fans." He looked at Abigail, not just at her but through her. He was beyond angry. "And I guess I'll wear something blue since they are the fighting blue sharks and all. Yes, okay thank you."

Liam hung up the phone and went to the bedroom. He threw some clothes in a bag and walked back to the living room where Abigail was sitting dumbfounded. "I'm going to Ted's for the night. I'll be back sometime tomorrow. Please watch over Aoife. Have a good night, Abi."

Abigail tried to grab his arm to make him stay and talk. She had no idea why her school had won. She hadn't entered them in the contest. At this point, she didn't think he would believe her, but she had to try. "Liam, wait! Let's talk about this. I swear to you I did NOT enter my school. There must be some mistake."

Liam pulled his arm away. "But you blogged about it. I saw it. So why shouldn't I believe that you entered? You should see if you can change your flight to tomorrow. I'll pay the difference. I'll see you in a month for your students' performance." With that, Liam walked out the door.

Abigail crumbled to the floor and cried. Aoife came and climbed on her lap. She gave her sweet kitty kisses trying to cheer her up. It only made Abigail cry harder.

Ryan's car wasn't there when Liam arrived. He was very glad for that. He knocked on the door. Connie was quick to open it. She had a feeling something like this might be how the night ended. She gave Liam a hug.

"Can I crash in your spare room?" Liam let out a loud sigh.

"Of course, come on in. Ted has some scotch in his office already waiting for you."

Liam snorted. "So, you were expecting me."

Connie shrugged. "I also have wine in the kitchen. Just in case it was Abi.

Liam's face hardened at the sound of her name. "In the office you said?"

Connie nodded and Liam headed towards the office. She sighed as she double checked the locks, turned off extra lights and headed for bed. She had a feeling Ted and Liam would be up for a while talking.

Abigail woke up to a cat curled up by her head. The sun was streaming through the window like it had done so many times before, but this time was different, there was no Liam, only the memory of him walking out the door and not coming back.

Abigail left Liam a note. She tried to explain everything. Part of her wasn't ready to give up on this relationship, and part of her was angry. Angry that he didn't believe her. That he didn't give her the chance to explain. Where was the understanding, the trust, the love?! She ripped the note in half and left it on the table, gave Aoife one last snuggle then grabbed her bag and waited outside for her uber driver to take her to the airport.

* * *

Liam woke up to the smell of bacon and coffee. He stretched, reaching over his head for Aoife. It was a knee jerk reaction by this point. He sighed when he realized she couldn't possibly be there. He got up and rambled into the kitchen to find Connie cooking breakfast. She handed him a cup of coffee before flipping the bacon. "How did you sleep?"

Liam took several sips of coffee then reached for the milk and sugar on the table. "I slept so-so."

"You know she loves you and didn't mean to hurt you right?" She handed him a bagel with cream cheese.

"And you know this from all the time you spent together being best friends, is that it?"

"Hey! She's a good person and you know it. She felt bad about keeping such a big secret from you. I could tell by the conversation we had. I could have gotten more but Ryan walked in."

"Gah! Ryan, he literally blew up my world last night. That guy is a peach!"

"Don't blame the messenger. Although he didn't really know what he was blowing up. He also didn't know when the hell to shut the hell up."

"I completely agree with that!" Ted walked into the kitchen. "Sorry about all of that, Liam."

"Not your fault, man."

Connie placed plates of food on the table. "I hate to mention it, but did you just leave Abi at your apartment? Have you talked to her since you got here?"

Liam shook his head.

"Liam! Don't be a tool. Call her right now. Or no more coffee for you!" Ted pulled Liam's coffee cup away from him.

"Fine! Fine!" Liam got up to make the call in the next room. He called but her phone went straight to voicemail. He called three times and got her voicemail every time. He came back into the kitchen and started eating his breakfast.

Connie looked from Liam to Ted and back again. "Well?!"

"I got her voice mail. Three times."

"So, that's it? You're done?"

Liam put down his fork and wiped his mouth. "I have no idea what anything means at the moment."

"But you still love her?"

Liam sighed. "Of course I do. I just need to figure out if I can get past this or not."

Connie gave Liam a hug. "Just remember fan really isn't a four-letter word no matter what Abi or you may think. You know what you have with her. So make your decision based on that."

Ted nodded his head in agreement. "She makes you shine bright, man."

Liam pushed his chair back. "Thanks for the bed, the breakfast and the chat. But I've got a relationship to save."

He left the kitchen and grabbed his bag, not bothering to change his clothes before he left. When he got home, he called out for Abigail. "Abi! You still here? Abi! We need to talk!" He looked around his apartment and saw Aoife sulking on the windowsill. He checked his bedroom, and her bag was gone. He saw the note ripped in half on his kitchen table. He taped it together and read it. He cursed under his breath. It was too late.

# CHAPTER TWENTY-FOUR

---

Abigail collapsed on her couch when she got home, leaving her bag at her door. Lochlan and Beatrice immediately crawled up on her and began sniffing her. They meowed in protest at their mom cheating on them with another cat. They could smell Aoife all over her. They quickly went to work rescenting their mother.

Tess brought her a cup of tea. "Maybe it's not over. I mean you did say he tried to call you. Maybe he's ready to talk."

Abigail sipped her tea as she shook her head. "That's great, but I'm not ready to talk to him. He treated me like—"

"Like someone who lied to him?" Tess dared to remark.

Abigail gave her a look of death. "There are two sides to every story you know, and he wouldn't even let me tell mine!"

Tess sat down next to Abigail on the couch. "Abi, you're my best friend and I'm on your side, really I am."

"But?" Abigail practically spat out.

"That's it. I love you and I'm on your side. But for now, I'm going to leave you alone. Before I go, I'll run a bath for you. When you get out, there will be some warm food on the stove for you. Please, take some time to enjoy the bath. You need to relax and decompress. Then eat something and go to bed. Things will look different in the morning."

Abigail just nodded. Tess got the bath ready and then brought her into the bathroom. "It's all set, so just enjoy. Food will be in the kitchen when you are ready." Tess closed the door behind her. She went to the kitchen to make something for Abigail to eat and then headed out. She would call Abigail in the morning.

Abigail stripped down and slipped into the warm water. It was lavender scented. Tess had even lit some candles and put them on the sink counter. Abigail just relaxed in the water and let herself cry. She had made such a mess of things and she had solidified it by not returning his phone calls. It was fine. She had her students to think about and her animals at the shelter who needed her. Maybe she would add another volunteer day to her schedule. She had a life before Liam, and she would have one after.

What she really needed to do was to decide if she was going to keep her blog going. She loved *EverMorphs*. She didn't want what had happened with Liam to ruin it for her, like Ryan had with *Lost Continent.* Tonight wasn't the time to make any big decisions though. Abigail got out of the tub and dried off. She put on some comfy jammies and headed into the kitchen to see what Tess had left her. Abigail laughed when she lifted the pot on the stove and saw a note. *'Gurl! You know I can't cook with what you have in your kitchen! Pizza should arrive in the next ten minutes. Love you! - Tess'*

Abigail walked into the living room and made herself comfortable on her couch and turned on a movie. Lochlan and Beatrice hopped up, made a few circles and curled up next to her, one on each side. She absentmindedly pet both of them as she stared at the television, not really watching the movie that was on. She was brought out of her haze by the sound of her door buzzer. She got up and opened the door for the delivery person. Tess had already paid and tipped. Abigail thanked the delivery person and took the pizza back to the living room. Pepperoni and bacon, her favorite, especially with the added bonus of a stuffed cheese crust.

Abigail pulled at the crust, giving bits of cheese to the cats. When she finished, she put the remains in her fridge and headed to bed. She curled up with her favorite stuffed animal. It was a teddy bear that her older sister had given her for her fifth birthday. It wasn't as fully stuffed as it used to be and one of the eyes was missing, but it always gave her comfort. She didn't realize how exhausted she was until her head hit the pillow and her eyelids became too heavy to raise. She spent the night sleeping and dreaming of Liam. She was on one side of the cliff, and he was on the other with a great, deep chasm in between them.

* * *

Liam tossed and turned the entire night until finally at four a.m, he gave up and went into the living room. Aoife followed him. He went into the kitchen to turn on the kettle. He had to be up in an hour to get ready for work anyway, so he figured he might as well get a head start. Irish breakfast tea should be the perk he needed before a morning jog. He fed Aiofe and gave her an extra scoop of wet food mixed in with her dry. He could tell she was missing Abigail, almost as much as he was.

Liam sighed as he headed into his bedroom to put on some jogging clothes. He sat on his bed and laughed out loud. He hated jogging, always had. But he felt it was a fitting punishment for how his week had ended and he needed a little physical pain to match emotional pain. Thirty minutes later, his wish was granted when his left calf cramped up as he was running. He knew it was a sign his day was not going to go well. He drove up to the set and his suspicions were confirmed when he pulled up to his trailer and Bianca Monroe was leaning against it with a smug little smile on her face.

Liam pinched the bridge of his nose as he got out of the car and took off his sunglasses. "Hello Bianca, why are you here?" He tried to be as cordial as he could.

"They don't let just anyone on set you know." Bianca twirled her sunglasses in her hand.

Liam moved past her and entered his trailer shutting the door behind him. Bianca opened it, making herself comfortable.

"You're here early."

"And how would you know that? You've been off the show for two years now. So again I ask you, why are you here?"

"I'm here because I was given the distinct honor of being the first to tell you that I am back!"

Liam gave Bianca a look. "What do you mean back?"

"I'm back on the show for the last two episodes of this season and the first half of the next season. That's all I said yes to so far." Bianca moved in and ran her hand along Liam's chest. "We'll have to see how things go."

Liam grabbed Bianca's hand and pushed it away. "Things with us are going nowhere. Remember? That was your decision. Too late to take it back now."

Bianca stood up a little straighter. She was ready for the pushback. But she knew what she wanted and why she had really returned to the show. "We'll see about that. You just need to get used to me being back. Oh, and I'll be going to that school drama thing in Connecticut with you."

Liam was stunned as he shook his head. "Excuse me?"

Bianca scoffed. She had forgotten how naive Liam could be about the business. It surprised her since he was so popular and fully ingrained in the machine. "Did you really think it was all about getting the arts back in schools? Maybe a little, but it's a huge publicity stunt to announce me coming back to the show."

"Can you please leave? I need to get ready for my work today."

Bianca nodded. "Of course. I don't start for two more days. I just wanted to give you a couple of days to take in the idea of me being around again." She winked, gave her long jet black hair a flip, and sauntered out of his trailer.

Liam collapsed on the couch, immediately calling Arlene. "Leenie! Bianca! Really?!"

Arlene cringed. She hadn't even said hello yet. She was really hoping she would get to him before she did.

"I can handle working with her again. But her busting in on the school event. Especially with how things went down with Abi."

"Wait, what happened with Abi?"

Liam went to tell her most of the horribleness of Abigail's visit, ending with the fact he hoped to mend things at the event., But with Bianca going that would be impossible.

Arlene knew Liam couldn't see her, but she stood up and vehemently started shaking her head as she paced around her desk. "NO! You don't let Bianca waylay you in any way, shape or form! You hear me! You will go to that event and you will get your woman back! Look, Abi is the best, and I do mean the best, thing that has happened to you since you got cast on *The EverMorphs*. And I won't let you throw all that away. So, she's a fan, and didn't tell you. Who gives a flying fig! She isn't crazy, she's not a diva or a bitch. She's intelligent, funny, charismatic, sassy, loving, and most of all head over heels about you! Have you even read the blog that Ryan found?"

Liam sighed. "I have read some of it, and it's actually pretty awesome." He shook his head as he chuckled. "I'm an idiot."

"Not an idiot, just cautious, and rightly so. But Abi is the real deal."

"Can you possibly arrange it so that I can fly in ahead of Bianca? And can you come too? I'm going to need your help with something."

Arlene smiled. "Now that's the Liam I know and love! Of course I'll even book us first class seats. The studio can foot the bill since they hired that witch Bianca back. They owe you one."

Liam laughed. "I don't know about that."

"Ha! You let me worry about it. It's my superpower."

# CHAPTER TWENTY-FIVE

❖————————————❖

*And That's All I Have To Say About That!*

*All Things EverMorph All the Time*

*S*eason 4 Episode Highlights - WINGS!! Lowlight - Who has Flint? Spill already!!!*

*Greetings and Salutations, my ever faithful Everrites and Morphlings. I know it's been a minute. My humblest apologies, I had a personal glitch that overtook me for a moment, but I'm back! And wow, Wow, WOW!!!*

*Can we all just take a moment and relish in the joy of WINGS!! So many fabulous characters got wings!! And I have to say both Everrites and Morphlings alike should be happy with the doling out of the wings. It's pretty even and pretty spectacular on both sides. Now, although we haven't seen him in a minute, which is my next pet peeve I'll discuss shortly, I believe Flint has wings as well. Maybe* someday soon we'll find out. So I want to know, who are you most excited about having wings? Who do you wish had wings and doesn't? And most importantly do you think anyone is hiding their wings?

Okay, back to Flint! Dear sweet, kidnapped Flint. We all know someone has him. We all know that someone is BAD! However, can the bad Flint kidnapping freak please step out from behind the shadows and reveal themselves! I mean come on! The season is only twelve episodes long! There are only two left! Don't wait until the end of the twelfth episode to tell us. Sadly, I think that is EXACTLY what will happen. Grrrr!!! Any thoughts? At first, I thought it was Oberon, but I've thrown that scenario out the window. Now, I'm flirting with the idea of Zarina. But if it's her, I think she is working with someone. I just can't figure out who.

So, do you agree? Disagree? Share your theories and thoughts. I love hearing them all!

Until next time EternallyEvers OUT!!

Comments: **IFollowFlint:** Glad to see you back EE! You were missed! <3. Of course Flint has wings! At least that's what I believe. But where the hell is he? I like your guess of Zarina. I definitely think it's a woman.

> **NylaKingdom4Ever:** Why doesn't the queen have wings? I mean out every fairy shouldn't she have them the most?!
>
> Reply: **IdolofIsla:** Lochlan has them. Maybe they skip a generation?

* * *

Abigail was getting back in the swing of her life. It had been three weeks since her trip and she was finally beginning to feel herself again. She had squashed any rumors with her students by threatening pop quizzes every week if they kept speculating. The year was beginning to wind down. The play was only a week and a half away. Margot was frantic with last minute assistant director duties. Abigail was very proud of her taking on such a big responsibility. She would miss having her in her classes, but she knew NYU was lucky to be getting such a great student next fall.

Principal Edwards walked into one of their final rehearsals with a rather large package in her arms. "I'm sorry to interrupt, but I have a special delivery for you Miss Reese, and your drama students."

Abigail gathered the students to the edge of the stage. "What is it, Principal Edwards?"

"It seems you have won some kind of contest and several actors from the hit show *The EverMorphs* are coming to see you all perform."

The students started squealing and talking amongst themselves. Trying to figure out when they would be coming and what they wanted to have signed. Some of the girls wanted to make salon appointments to get a mani-pedi and their hair done before the special guests made their appearance. The majority of the drama club were fans of the show.

Principal Edwards pulled Abigail aside. "I wish you had mentioned that you had entered this contest and that winning was a possibility. I've been on the phone with the superintendent most of the day trying to figure out the logistics of all of this. They are coming next week you know."

"I'm sorry Mrs. Edwards, but I can honestly say I didn't enter this contest." She turned and looked at Margot, then back to Principal Edwards. "However, I have an idea of who did, but I have no proof yet."

"We can worry about that later. I've got another meeting with the school board and a representative from the show. I'll have more details for you as I get them. Just make sure the students are ready." With that Principal Edwards left, leaving Abigail to deal with the multitude of questions.

Once Abigail finished rehearsal and left the kids with a vow of silence until the announcement was made in the paper, her thoughts turned to how she would deal with Liam next week. Even though he had reached out several times, she had ignored him. A clean break was what she thought she wanted and more importantly needed. It had been a long time since she had opened up like that, the pain of a break-up always seemed to take a little bit of her soul. She shook her head trying to get back to concentrating on the students in front of her. She knew her mind was wandering so she got out her famous 'change it' bell and rang it.

The students immediately stopped working on their reading assignment and put their books away. They knew the 'change it' bell meant they were about to do something out of the box and usually very creative and very fun.

"What's the twist today, Miss Reese?"

"Today we are going to tell each other one mythical creature you wish was real. In fact, you have one as a pet and I want to hear all about it."

The class looked at each other. This was a new one for Miss Reese. "Any mythical creature?" Margot asked.

"Can we make one up?" Andrew wanted to know.

Abigail stood up to get her egg timer. "Absolutely! Okay, I'll give you all fifteen minutes. Once we all share, we'll vote and the best one gets to decide what baked good I bring you all tomorrow."

The class reacted positively and immediately began talking to each other about what kind of mystical creature they would want or would invent. The buzzer went off and fifteen hands shot in the air each wanting to be the first to share their creature.

The room phone went off and the class gave a collective groan. Abigail went to answer it. "Hello?"

"Hello Miss Reese, the principal would like you to come down after this period. She wants to discuss the logistics of the contest coverage. And please bring Margot Midsnow with you."

"Thank you, Estelle. We'll be there." Abigail turned back to see her class all listening intently, hoping their fun wasn't being interrupted for an office visit. "Alright, who wants to go first?" Abigail smiled.

The rest of class flew by and just as the results were tallied the bell rang. No one moved. They wanted to know what they would be having tomorrow. "The winner is Connor, with his half pegasus, quarter lion, and quarter dragon pet Nimsy. What treat would you like tomorrow for the class?"

Connor looked around the class. And they nodded. Clearly there had been a hushed conversation around the topic. "We would like your sin sticks please." Connor had the biggest grin on his face.

Her students had gotten her good. She had only made sin sticks once because they were labor intensive. It was basically a shish kabob that had caramel peanut brownie squares, rice krispy treat squares and chocolate covered marshmallow squares. Each one had different coverings and candy decorations. Abigail put her hands in the air. "Okay, you got me, but you have to give me two days."

The class nodded in agreement as they gathered their things and headed out the door. Abigail stopped Margot. "Hang back a minute."

The class filed out and Margot took a seat. "Is everything okay?"

"Oh yes, everything is fine. We just need to go to the office. Principal Edwards wants to see us. It's about the contest logistics."

Margot relaxed. "Oh, good. I'm so excited!" They headed out the door and down to the office. Principal Edwards was waiting for them in her office.

"Now, I know you must be so excited for the prize and it will be a nice boost for the school image, but I have to say I wish whoever decided to do this had passed this by me before deciding to enter. Especially since this event is so close to the end of the year. We have a lot going on already with prom and graduation only a month away. Did you ever figure out who it was, Miss Reese?"

Abigail started to speak but Margot stopped her. "It's my fault, Mrs. Edwards. Miss Reese didn't enter the contest, I did. And she didn't know I had done it. Some friends and I took it upon ourselves, we thought it would be fun to enter. We didn't actually think we would win, that's why I didn't ask. Better to ask forgiveness than permission, right?" Margot shrugged.

Principal Edwards couldn't help but laugh. "You are learning fast, young lady. But Margot, sometimes forgiveness has consequences. Luckily for you Miss Reese already had a suspicion it was you and told me. She also asked me to let your questionable judgment slide this one time."

Margot locked down and bit her lip. "Thank you Mrs. Edwards, and again, I'm sorry."

Abigail changed the subject, "I was thinking to make things easier we could have them come to the final dress rehearsal? That way it's closed except to the cast and crew. We can allow them to invite their family but that's it."

Principal Edwards nodded her head. "I like that idea. I've been told only one television crew, BCA, has an exclusive, just one camera person and a reporter. I believe a couple of photographers from some magazines and the local newspaper will be here as well."

"Wow! I'm going to feel like I'm famous!" Margot gushed.

"Now do you wish you had auditioned?" Abigail raised an eyebrow at Margot.

Margot shook her head. "No! It would be too much pressure." Margot turned to the principal. "Mrs. Edwards, can you tell me who exactly is coming? I mean from the cast."

Principal Edwards pulled up the email with all the information on her computer. She used her reading glasses to search for the names. "It looks like three cast members will be joining us. Liam Caffney, Lara Burnesta, and TBD. It's a surprise cast member with a special announcement of some sort."

"Maybe they will tell us the release date for the next season." Margot mused. "Or better yet a trailer for next season!"

"Hold your horses there, I seriously doubt it would be a trailer. If that was the case they would have asked for special equipment to pull that off and from what I've seen they haven't asked for anything except for some microphones." Principal Edwards shut down Margot's notions quickly.

Abigail tried to make her feel better. "It's probably just an additional cast member they can't reveal because their appearance hasn't been confirmed by the actor yet. Let's just be happy for the two confirmed and we'll be surprised by the possibility of a third."

Margot nodded in agreement. She felt the need to be on her best behavior for the time being.

# CHAPTER TWENTY-SIX

L iam fidgeted in his seat the entire time on the plane. The last week at work had been brutal. Having Bianca back on set had been traumatic to say the least. Liam had spent most of his free time with Ted and Connie. Ted couldn't believe she was back, and Connie had suddenly not had any time to help Bianca locate new housing. Liam was so grateful for them. He had stopped himself so many times from calling Abigail. He had left enough messages that she didn't return, so he was finally taking the hint. But he wasn't ready to give up. He had even sent more flowers to the shelter but the delivery had been declined by Steve. He was about to take a big gamble and he prayed it would pay off.

Arlene reached out her hand and gave his hand a squeeze. "Relax, whatever happens happens. You've done all you can."

Liam nodded, taking a few deep breaths. "You're right. You're right. This should be fine. I should be fine. We should be fine." He hoped the next part of his plan would not backfire. He knew he would find out tomorrow morning.

Arlene hit the button for the flight attendant. "You need a drink, and so do I."

* * *

Abigail got home to find a package waiting for her at her door. She took it into the living room then went back to the kitchen to check on the cats' food and water. She gave them fresh water. Then opened the fridge to see what she was going to make for dinner. She had some leftovers she could reheat. Pizza sounded better so she ordered one from her favorite pizza place in town. She got fancy and added artichoke hearts, bacon and tomatoes to it this time. She poured herself a glass of red wine and went to her living room to watch some DTV. Lochlan and Beatrice took their usual spots at her side, purring as they snuggled close.

Abigail reached for the package and opened it. It was a telescope. Small enough to sit nicely on her balcony and give her a good view of the stars. There was a note inside that read *'Some people think I'm a star. But in truth you Abigail, are mine. I'm sorry, let's talk, please.'* She smiled at the note and the present. Maybe he was ready to accept all that she was, including her being a fan. She wasn't completely ready to step back in, so she just left him a text. It said 'Thank You.' Nothing more and nothing less. She would see Liam in two days. That gave her two more days to figure out what if anything she wanted to say to him. The door buzzer took her out of her thoughts of Liam. Her dinner had arrived.

The following morning, Abigail got to work early. Her first period seniors were doing presentations on a character they had chosen to research from *The Canterbury Tales*. She was loaded with licorice, both black and red, and carrot sticks. She found giving them something to crunch before the presentations began helped to ease the tension of the students. And she would give them a break every three students to have some licorice. There was something about working the jaw. She had added another element this time. Chamomile tea. It had helped her calm down many times so she would offer it to her students if they wanted to try some. She had also brought some lavender oil to put in her diffuser. Lavender was a known calming flower. The room would be prepared by the time her students got there.

Her students filed in and took their seats. "What's that smell?" Keith asked.

"It's lavender," Abigail remarked.

"I like it." Keith nodded in approval.

"Okay, everyone take your seats please. Today we are going to do it *Hunger Games* style. Everyone's name is in this bowl." Abigail picked up a bowl to show the class. "I'll draw a name and that's who will present first."

"Can we pick the first name?" Liam smiled as he and Lara entered the room with Principal Edwards and Arlene.

"Oh shit!" Amanda yelled.

"Language!" Principal Edwards pointed at Amanda.

"Sorry Mrs Edwards, but it's Lochlan and Queen Ryla!"

Lara laughed. "Please call me Lara, and this is the handsome Liam. Sorry for interrupting but we wanted to meet Margot, Miss Reese and all the rest of the class. Your letter captured our hearts and we just had to find out more about all of you."

Principal Edwards pulled Abigail aside. "Sorry for the ambush. They just showed up this morning. They made a compelling argument. It's just for this class. And then tomorrow will go as scheduled."

"Oh, it's fine. Just look at my students. They are in heaven."

"I'll leave you to it then." Principal Edwards smiled and headed out the door.

"So, which one of you is Margot?" Liam asked as he walked around the room. He was careful not to make direct eye contact with Abigail, but he did watch her out of the corner of his eye.

"And who has some of those amazing stickers on hand so I can get a closer look?" Lara questioned.

Amanda's hand shot right up. "I'm not Margot but I have the stickers. All of them are on my binder here." She handed her binder to Lara.

"I'm Margot." She tentatively stood up.

"Ah! Sweet Margot!" Liam walked up to her and gave her a big hug. "Thank you for sending the letter."

"I wanted to surprise Miss Reese. She's my favorite teacher and I think she likes the show, even if she won't admit it."

"Is that right?" Liam looked at Abigail and smiled. "Well, I know that we at *EverMorphs* would be honored to have a fan as wonderful and special as Miss Reese. We hear what a wonderful teacher she is. That she is kind and wise. That she knows how to make you laugh and feel like you are the most important person in the room. She listens and is caring and gives all of herself without asking for anything in return. And most importantly she is someone you can trust without question." Liam kept eye contact with Abigail the entire time he was speaking even though he was walking around the room.

"She's the best!" Megan yelled out. The class started clapping in agreement.

"Well, it seems there is a Queen in this realm of English learning, my son," Lara proclaimed.

"'Tis true mother. And they deserve a space in the kingdom of Nyla. Wouldn't you agree?" Liam gave a royal bow before his mother the queen.

"I think it only fair to make them all honorary kinsmen of the fairy realm of Nyla. So shall it be!" Lara waved her hand up in great fanfare.

Liam excused himself from the room for a moment and came back with two very large bags filled with sweatshirts and water bottles for everyone in the class. "Please accept these humble tokens as remembrance of this day and your kinship to our realm." Liam and Lara started hanging out the sweatshirts and bottles.

Margot got hers first and looked it over very carefully. "Is this swag for next season?" She was shocked.

Liam nodded. "We may have twisted a few arms to get this, but yes this is brand new, no one has seen it yet official *EverMorphs* merchandise for season five."

The room erupted in cheers. Abigail tried to quiet them down, as she kept the tears brimming at the edge of her eyes at bay. She was well aware Liam had been speaking directly to her. "Class, come on now. Bring it down a notch or two."

Lara clapped her hands. "Now, who wants pictures?

Everyone reached for their phones.

"Alright let's just go row by row for individual pictures and then we'll do a big group shot, sound good?" Lara suggested.

"That sounds great," Abigail agreed. "Keith and Connor, can you help move some desks so we can have a good wall to take photos against?"

The boys quickly went to work with Lara guiding them. Liam walked over to Abigail. He gave her a tentative smile. "Hi."

"Hi," she said back.

"It's good to see you. You look wonderful," Liam commented. "I've missed you."

Abigail took a step back. "Thank you for the telescope, it's lovely."

"You are very welcome. How are Cassiopeia and Dipper?"

Abigail grimaced. "They are good. I think they miss you. But you should know their names are actually Lochlan and Beatrice."

Liam laughed out loud a little louder than he expected. It surprised Abigail. "That's why they never came when I called them. I thought they just didn't like me!" Liam took a step closer to Abigail. "Can we have dinner tonight and talk?"

Abigail nodded. "That would be nice."

"I'll make reservations somewhere quiet."

Abigail hesitated for a moment. "No, why don't you come to my place? I'll make food or order out. But it will be an easier place to talk."

Liam was relieved. He wanted to talk at her apartment, but he didn't want to presume anything. That's why he had suggested a quiet restaurant. "Is seven o'clock alright?"

Abigail smiled. "Sounds good." Abigail looked around the room. "It looks like they are ready for pictures. Are you ready for them?"

"As long as you're by my side I am ready for anything." Liam gave her hand a squeeze and walked away before she could say anything else.

The school was buzzing with news of the celebrity visit for the rest of the day. Abigail's students were either walking on cloud nine or completely bummed that they weren't seniors yet and had missed the big event. Abigail had to admit she was really happy about what Liam had done. Principal Edwards had told her about the ambush he and Lara had made. He even made a donation to the drama club to sweeten the deal. He was trying, and she appreciated it. Even if he was throwing his money and clout around just a little bit to do it.

After school she had a quick meeting with her drama students so they would all know what was happening the next day and so Margot could get the last family head count for attendance. Once that was done, she headed to the grocery store to pick up a few things. Taco salads were yummy and simple. She would also whip up a quick sin brownie. She was basically just taking the brownie part of one of her sin sticks. This brownie would have a layer of caramel and peanut in the middle and be topped with a toasted marshmallow topping. Baking helped her relax and she most definitely needed to relax.

Abigail knew she wanted to get back together with Liam, but she didn't want to be hurt again. Part of her wanted nothing more to do with him, but the bigger part of her wanted him in her life now and forever. She had to ask herself if she was willing to risk maybe getting hurt again. Baking helped her think clearly.

With a clear head and a freshly showered body, Abigail put her hair in a high ponytail and put some music on. She was pouring two glasses of wine, the same wine they had on their very first date when the door buzzer went off. She didn't even answer, just buzzed Liam in. A minute later there was a knock on her door.

Abigail opened the door to find Liam with a bouquet of peonies mixed with mums, two of her favorite flowers. Closing her eyes, she took a big whiff. They smelled like peace and tranquility. "Thank you, they are beautiful." She stepped aside and Liam came in.

"I tried to call you. I left some messages." He wasn't being judgmental or accusatory. He was just speaking his mind.

"I wasn't ready to talk." Abigail handed him the glass of wine. "But I listened to every message."

Liam took a sip and smiled. "It's our wine."

She pulled out a chair. "Dinner is ready."

They made small talk as they ate. Much like they did on their first date. It was relaxing for both of them.

"Dessert in the living room?" Abigail suggested.

"Let me help with the dishes." Liam stood up and cleared the table.

Abigail took his hand in hers. "We can wash them later." She brought him into the living room and sat him on the couch. "I'll be right back." A few minutes later she came back with two big pieces of brownie with some vanilla bean ice cream on the side. She had warmed the brownie slightly so the ice cream was the perfect kind of melty.

Liam took his and tasted it. "Mmm, this is delicious, Abi." He put it down and looked at her. "Abi, I think we should—"

"Get back together," Abigail finished his sentence.

"Really? Is that what you want? Because that's what I want. I'm so sorry I acted like a big jerk. I needed time to process, and I needed a smack in the head from two very wise and very happy people."

Abigail nodded. She made a mental note to thank Ted and Connie. "And you're alright with me being a fan? I mean have you read my blog? I'm a pretty big one. And I won't give it up."

"If you don't hide your fandom from me. I will fully embrace it. It's part of you, and I love all of you."

"And I love all of you." Abigail put her arms around Liam as he pulled her into a kiss, bringing her body as close to his as possible. It was familiar yet somehow new territory. They were gently forced apart by a cat slinking in between them.

Liam looked down and scooped up the cat. "It's lovely to meet you again, Beatrice." That cat mewed and crawled up his chest resting in the middle. She curled into a little ball and began purring.

Abigail laughed. "I knew she missed you."

"What do you think of the name *LovelyLochlanLocks*?"

Abigail was puzzled. She reached for one of Liam's curls and twirled it around her fingers. "It's an interesting name. Did you read it somewhere?"

Liam gave a devilish smile. "Nope."

"Is it someone I should be looking out for?" Abigail kissed his neck.

Liam nodded. "Absolutely. I think he'll have some insightful comments for your blog." He moved Beatrice off of his chest.

Abigail raised an eyebrow. "He? Really? You think it's him?"

"I know it is." Liam leaned in and kissed her. "I also know that you really like the way he does this." Liam gave her neck a little lick and a gentle bite. It sent a delicious shiver up and down her spine.

She sighed, trying not to moan. "I can't wait to see what other surprises he has for me."

Liam winked. "Let me show you."

# CHAPTER TWENTY-SEVEN

"I can't believe you made me fly alone." Bianca pouted as she got into the limousine she was taking to the school with the others.

"I can't believe you thought it would be any other way." Liam snorted.

"Children, be nice," Lara admonished. She sighed wishing that Bianca was not at the event. She had a way of sucking the joy out of events.

"And what's this all about?" Bianca shoved a photo from their school visit on Self-Site in Arlene's face.

Arlene pushed the phone away. "It was a private event Liam had planned. You weren't invited."

"Clearly!" Bianca settled back in her seat. "I wouldn't have minded some free publicity you know. "

"I didn't do it for publicity. I did it to be nice. You should try that sometime."

Bianca opened her mouth then closed it when she saw the look Lara was giving her. She knew she needed to be careful. Her agent had worked miracles to get her back on the show and she knew it was a slippery slope. But the rest of the cast didn't need to know that. And she was only in phase one of her plan to get Liam back. So far her plan had not been going well, but she wasn't sure why. She had seen pictures of Liam with some fat woman but those had been weeks ago and she knew it couldn't have been anything but a friendship. Filters did wonders to make pictures look like things they couldn't possibly be, so that couldn't be the reason. She just needed to keep trying. They rode the rest of the ride in silence.

The school auditorium was buzzing with the activities. A special section had been roped off for the photographers, and reporters. Another section was for the families of the students involved in the show, and the last section was for the three special guests. Margot was calm but resolved as she ran around backstage making sure everyone had everything they needed. It was fifteen minutes to curtain.

Flashes went off as the actors walked into the auditorium and down the aisle, especially when they saw Bianca Monroe squeezing close to Liam. Their explosive red carpet break up was no surprise to the press and had been headline gold for several weeks. To see them walking in together made the press salivate with possibilities.

They headed straight to the stage, as Arlene went to the roped off section where they would be sitting to watch the show. Quickly the audience quieted themselves as they found their way to their seats and sat down.

Principal Edwards walked on from off stage right, meeting up with the actors center stage. She shook all their hands and then faced the audience. "We are honored and privileged to have stars Liam Caffney, Lara Burnesta, and Bianca Monroe from the hit television series *The EverMorphs* joining us for this special invite dress rehearsal of our drama club's production of *Merry Widows, Merry Brides,* directed by Abigail Reese and Margot Midsnow. The arts are such a vital part of the education system and moments like these help insure and remind us of what could be. Now, without further adieu, let me introduce Mr. Liam Caffney." Principal Edwards gave the microphone to Liam and then started clapping. The audience followed suit.

Liam gave a small bow. "Thank you so much for having us this Saturday afternoon. I know I speak for myself and my fellow cast mates when I tell you we are honored and humbled to be here. I know we all got bit by the acting bug through our school arts programs, and I for one am excited to see these young people keep the spark of the arts alive." He handed the mike to Lara.

"And to that end we will be giving these wonderful students some tips and tricks of the trade after their performance today to take with them into their shows tomorrow and the next couple of weeks." She handed the mike to Bianca.

"The show received a massive amount of requests but the one written by Margot Midsnow touched all of our hearts. I'm a little late to the game and only read the letter yesterday but it truly touched me and I couldn't let this day pass without giving Margot a hug. Margot, can you come out here please?"

Margot came out from behind the curtain and hesitantly made her way to Bianca. Bianca put her arm around her. "Thank you for loving *The EverMorphs*, your teacher and your school so much. In honor of you bearing it all to us, I have some news to bear to you right here and right now. You are the first to know. Are you ready for the secret?" Bianca looked to the audience and then back to Margot. Margot nodded. "Come next season Mortals and Fae alike better be prepared because Kortalina is back!"

There was an audible gasp from the students backstage.

Bianca laughed. "That's right! I'll be back on *The EverMorphs* for season five. And who knows what kind of havoc my character will wreak."

A reporter leapt up from her seat. "Does that mean you and Liam are an item again?"

"Well." Bianca smiled and put her hand out for Liam to take.

He grabbed the mike out of her other hand instead. "No, we are not an item. I am in a committed relationship with someone I love." Liam went off stage and grabbed Abigail's hand. She stood in place refusing to move. "Come out with me, please. I want the world to know." Liam pulled.

"Are you sure?"

Liam squeezed her hand. "Absolutely."

Abigail kept holding his hand as he went back out on stage. He gave Abigail a kiss in front of everyone. More flashes went off.

"I knew it!" Margot yelped triumphantly.

Liam gave Margot a wink, and then looked at Bianca and shrugged. "But I look forward to sharing the screen with her again."

Bianca played it off like she meant to hand the mike to Liam all along.

Liam gave her a slight bow before turning back to the audience. "And now, I believe it's showtime! Places! Here we go!"

# EPILOGUE

＊━━━━━━━━＊

*And That's All I Have To Say About That!*

*All Things EverMorph All the Time*

*Season 4  SEASON FINALE!!*

*O h my dear sweet Everrites and Morphlings. Am I the only one completely blown away? How in the world am I supposed to last until next season! This is what a ring of purgatory must feel like. Alright, who's going to be starting a countdown calendar with me?*

*Okay, I can't go on a minute longer without saying Holy Hanna. Kortalina is back!!! Yes, yes, we all knew and expected her to be back next season, BUT SHE CAME BACK THIS SEASON!!! And I must admit I need to give myself a pat on the back or at least half a pat, because I was right about Zarina and*

*I was right about her working with someone. However, I had NO CLUE it was Kortalina she was in cahoots with. Did you? Come on, be honest!*

*Oh, and poor Flint, that evil Kortalina sucking his Fae essence dry. I can't wait until Lochlan rescues him and gives dear old Korti a who now and a what for! And he's sooooo close! Only a flight of stone steps away. Why? Why are they making us wait until next season for the rescue! Curse you EverMorph writers for being too damn good at your jobs! But we will have the entire break to contemplate what might befall our favorites next season. Anyone want to take a gander? Spill it, share your thoughts. And have no fear, I and this blog will not be going anywhere during the break. We have too much to unpack and too much to celebrate. For instance, who is going to Sci Con this summer? Anyone? Anyone?*

*Before I sign off please give a warm EverMorph welcome to LochlansLovelyLocks. I hope you feel at home and part of the family. We are all fans and friends here. Welcome!*

*Until next time EternallyEvers OUT!!*

# A Moment in EverMorph

Lochlan pushed his way through the mirror quickly, closing it behind him so that no others from his realm could follow or hear his words. He flicked the light switch up and down, no electricity. A flash of lightning zig zagged across the sky, illuminating the room. His wings bristled at the sound. He deposited his sword and dagger on the bed and headed out of the room in search of Beatrice. He knew she should be within her dwelling at this time.

Lochlan found Beatrice shivering at the front door. She had just locked it behind and was drenched from head to toe. A loud crack of thunder struck, making her cringe and yelp.

"Beatrice! Are you okay?" Lochlan moved to embrace her, not caring how wet she was. His winged enveloped her for a moment, cocooning her in a shield of warmth and love. A moment later his wings were folded back, and she was completely dry.

Beatrices smiled as she touched her dry clothes and hair. "Thank you for that. The storm seems to be getting worse, and it just came out of nowhere. It was sunny and warm only two hours ago."

Lochlan led her to the kitchen. "Come, let's get something warm within you."

She followed without question. "There are flash floods happening everywhere. I barely made it home. My car is a few blocks back. I couldn't safely drive it any further. Wait, what are you doing here? We weren't supposed to meet up for another two days."

"I had to come. There has been a shift, and everything is changing. I fear mortal time on this plane is running out."

Beatrice searched his eyes for answers. "What is it? What happened?"

"Kortalina has returned and she has taken Flint as her prisoner. She is the one wreaking havoc on your weather here, and she is draining Flint to do it."

"How is that possible? I thought the queen had banished her several years ago."

Lochlan held his head down in despair. He had yet to find his best friend, his second in command. Flint had been missing for three weeks now. Lochlan didn't know how much longer Flint would last.

Beatrice cupped Lochlan's head in her hands and looked him in the eye. She pushed out love and comfort to him. Beatrice was special. She was more evolved than the average mortal. It was one of the things that drew Lochlan to her. One of the reasons he wanted to save her, and others like her. There was good in humanity, he saw it and so did his mother, the queen.

"You will find him. I have faith in you Lochlan, do not doubt for a moment your abilities or in Flint's determination to stay alive until you find him. He knows you are searching." She put her hand on his heart. "Feel that, and know it to be true."

Lochlan grabbed her into a passionate kiss. A forbidden kiss. They both knew he was betrothed to Isla. But their attraction kept growing. They had fought it for so long. But now with things in both realms reaching a pinnacle they could no longer deny their desire or passion for each other.

Duty, honor, and code ran through Lochlan's mind, forcing him to pull his lips away from Beatrice. "I'm sorry, I shouldn't have done that."

Beatrice took a step back. "I understand." She went to make some tea. "What can I do to help you?"

"Keep alert. The Morphling faction is growing by the hour. More and more are crossing over into your dimension. The sentinels are doing the best they can, but still they are jumping through." Lochlan sighed, shoulders slumping. "There is another portal."

"Another portal? And you don't know where?"

Lochlan shook his head. "No, my men have been unable to locate it."

"I can help look. I just need to know what anomalies I should be searching for." Beatrice ran to get her laptop in the living room. Lochlan followed.

"Beatrice, you helping me will only put you in more danger than you are already in. I would break if something happened to you." He reached out to touch her but pulled his hand back. She didn't notice because she was concentrating on her computer.

But the shadow in the corner had noticed. She had witnessed the kiss and she was sure to report it back to Isla. But first she wanted to see what else the human and Lochlan were up to. Nyx slowed her breathing even further, her pulse slow and steady. For now she would listen and then use the portal Lochlan had referred to. She doubted the human would be smart enough to realize the unknown portal was right under her nose.

* * *

Flint pushed against his restraints. The chains were finally beginning to pull away from the stone wall. He pulled as loudly as he dared, not wanting to alert the guards. He was weak but was digging deep within himself to break free. He knew Lochlan was looking for him, but he doubted he would find him here.

Kortalina had created a den of destruction between the realms. It was a new level of black magic that no one in Nyla had ever encountered. Living between the realms could drive one crazy. There were stories, legends. Flint never thought them to be true. Not until now. Fae would last longer than mortals but the danger was still very real, and very deadly. He had to escape before it was too late.

Flint was tired. Kortalina was draining his fae powers to enhance hers. She took much of his essence, yet always leaving just enough so he could rejuvenate before she drained him again. Even a fae as strong and magical as him could not last like that forever. Eventually he wouldn't be able to rejuvenate and his life force would go back to the cosmos of which it came. If that happened Nyla and most assuredly the human race were doomed.

Made in the USA
Columbia, SC
23 January 2022